The Secret

of the
Seven Crosses

Drumshee Timeline Series – Book 2

Cora Harrison taught primary school children in England for twenty-five years before moving to a small farm in Kilfenora, Co. Clare. The farm includes an Iron Age fort, with the remains of a small castle inside it, and the mysterious atmosphere of this ancient place gave Cora the idea for a series of historical novels tracing the survival of the ringfort through the centuries. *The Secret of the Seven Crosses* follows Cora's first book, *Nuala & her Secret Wolf.*

For the children of Inchovea School,
especially Michael James Malone and John McGrath

OTHER TITLES BY CORA HARRISON

Nuala & her Secret Wolf
Drumshee Timeline Series – Book 1

Coming Soon
The Secret of 1798
The Secret of Drumshee Castle

The Secret
of the
Seven Crosses

Drumshee Timeline Series – Book 2

CORA HARRISON

Illustrated by Orla Roche

WOLFHOUND PRESS
& in the US and Canada
The Irish American Book Company

First published 1997 by
WOLFHOUND PRESS Ltd
68 Mountjoy Square
Dublin 1
Tel: (353-1) 8740354
Fax: (353-1) 8720207

Published in the US and Canada by
The Irish American Book Company
6309 Monarch Park Place
Niwot, Colorado 80503
USA
Tel: (303) 530-4400
Fax: (303) 530-4488

British Library Cataloguing in Publication Data
A catalogue record for this book is available from the British Library.

ISBN 0-86327-616-4

10 9 8 7 6 5 4 3 2 1

Typesetting: Wolfhound Press
Cover illustration: Orla Roche
Cover Design: Estresso
Printed and bound by The Guernsey Press Co. Ltd, Guernsey,
Channel Islands

CHAPTER ONE

𝔍t was my grandfather who told me about the treasure of Kilfenora – said Rory, lowering his voice so much that Malachy and Mary had to lean forward to hear what he was saying. 'He told me that the monks of Kilfenora Abbey had a huge store of treasure which they hid, long ago, to keep it safe from raiders, but that the secret of where it's hidden has been lost for centuries. It was a wonderful treasure, he said; it was full of gold coins and jewels and silver and gold cups, and it was brought here from the east in great jars, taller than a man. The only thing anyone knew about the hiding place, *his* grandfather told him, was that the secret was written down in one of the books of Kilfenora Abbey.'

Malachy tossed another log on the fire and then looked up, his eyes shining. 'I might be able to find it,' he said proudly. 'I can read. I can read all the books in the abbey's Scriptorium. Perhaps I'll be able to discover the secret.'

Both Mary and Rory looked at him with astonishment and respect. In thirteenth-century Ireland, very few people could read.

'You must be very clever,' said Mary admiringly.

Malachy smiled at her. He had been a pupil at the abbey since he was five years old, and during those seven years he had seen hardly any girls – and certainly not one as pretty as Mary, with her black curls and her gentian-blue eyes.

'It's easy,' he said modestly. 'Now, I could never be a stone-carver like Rory. I don't think I'd have the strength.'

Rory and Mary don't look like brother and sister, Malachy thought. Rory, though only two years older than Malachy, was almost a foot taller, with broad shoulders and fair hair and a freckled face, while Mary was tiny and dark-haired.

Malachy had only met Rory for the first time that day, but it had been an important day for both of them. Malachy was twelve now, and he had learnt all that he needed to learn at the abbey school; tomorrow he was to start copying the wonderful books in the Scriptorium. Rory had arrived to help his master with the carving of seven stone crosses to be placed around the abbey. From the moment they had met, the two boys had been friends; and the abbot had said that they could share a little one-roomed thatched cottage, with a central hearth and a bed of straw on either side. To both of them it seemed a wonderful house; and to Mary, used to the continual noise and bustle of a big farming family, the cottage seemed like paradise on this wet September afternoon. She was reluctant to return home.

'Tell us how you came to Kilfenora, Malachy,' she said, trying to spin out the time before she had to leave.

'Well, my parents died when I was quite young,' said Malachy. 'Then, when I was five years old, our farm at Drumshee was attacked by cattle raiders and my two brothers were carried away.'

'How did you escape?' asked Rory.

'I stayed hidden,' said Malachy slowly.

'That was clever of you, when you were so young,' said Mary. 'Where did you hide?'

Malachy hesitated. This was something which he had kept a secret for the last seven years. He had not even told Brother Declan, who had been his friend and teacher for all that time.

He looked at Mary's blue eyes and at Rory's honest face and knew that he could trust them.

'I discovered a secret hiding place at Drumshee,' he said. 'It was in the middle of a field that we called the *cathair*, a place that was all full of big stones. One day, when I was about four, I crawled underneath a blackthorn bush and discovered a hole with a flight of stairs going down. At the bottom of the steps was an underground room, with a passageway leading out into another field, just beside our well and our cattle drinking place. I used to hide there from my brothers whenever they were in a temper with me, and I was there on the day that the cattle raiders came. I saw everything that happened.'

'What did you do?' gasped Mary.

'Well, I waited until they had long gone, and then I walked across to Kylemore, where my aunt lived. She brought me to Kilfenora, and the Brothers kept me and taught me to read and to write, and when I'm fourteen I'll become one of them.'

There was a silence, and then Mary began to get to her feet.

'I'd better be going,' she said reluctantly. 'Mother will be wondering where I got to. I really only meant to walk across with Rory and then go straight back.'

'Wait a while,' said Malachy eagerly. 'Let's go on talking about the treasure. Do you know anything else about it, Rory? What sort of book was the secret written in? It seems funny that the monks haven't discovered it. They're always reading the books and making copies of them. I'm sure they haven't found the treasure, because I know they're quite poor. The abbot told me that he wants to make the church bigger, but he hasn't enough money.'

'Well, I don't know much about books,' said Rory hesitantly. 'The only thing I do know about, really, is carving stone crosses, and I know you can put something there which will mean something else – like a fish means Jesus. Could it be hidden in some way, like that? It could be some sort of puzzle.'

8

'It could be, perhaps,' said Malachy slowly. He thought for a minute and then looked up, his eyes shining. 'Let's make a promise,' he said eagerly. 'We'll all keep thinking about the treasure, and listening to any stories about it, and looking everywhere, and I'll look in all the books that I can; and we'll all discuss anything we find out. And if we do find treasure, we'll share it between the three of us. Do you promise?'

'I promise,' said Mary softly.

'I promise to share the treasure of Kilfenora with my friend Malachy and my sister Mary,' said Rory, his half-broken voice sounding deep and strong for the first few words and then cracking to a squeak which made them all laugh.

It was probably because he was laughing so hard that Malachy heard nothing, or perhaps Rory's ears were sharper than his; but almost before he had finished speaking, Rory was off his stool and over to the door. The bottom half of the door was closed, but the top half had been left open to let in the air and the light. Rory leaned out and looked down the village street; then, with a sharp exclamation, he opened the bottom half of the door, darted out, and was around the corner in a flash.

'What is it?' asked Mary.

'Someone must have been listening,' said Malachy. 'I hope they didn't hear anything.'

Malachy wondered briefly whether he should go and help Rory, but he decided that there was no point. Rory would be able to manage just as well on his own. So he stayed at the doorway, peering down the wet street and listening for any sounds.

'Here comes Rory,' said Mary after a few minutes. 'At least he hasn't got into a fight.'

Rory was breathing hard. 'I lost him,' he said. 'He ducked into a house. It was a young fellow, about my age, with a sooty face and a leather apron.'

'That was Colm, the blacksmith's son,' said Malachy. 'He's always hanging around, listening outside doors. He's quite stupid, really. He doesn't understand much.'

'Do you think he heard?' asked Mary nervously.

'I think he probably heard, but it won't mean much to him. In any case, he can't read and Brother Declan would never let him near a book, so we don't need to worry.'

Mary stepped outside the door. 'I'd better go now,' she said. 'Will you come and see us next Sunday, Rory? Bring Malachy with you and Mother will make you both a good meal. I'll come again next week, and I'll teach you both how to cook. I'll weave some cloth to make cushions for the stools, too, and then you'll be really comfortable.'

'We'll walk back with you,' said Rory. 'I want to show Malachy where our farm is.'

CHAPTER TWO

When the two boys returned to the village, they saw an elderly monk coming towards them.

'That's Brother Declan,' said Malachy in a low voice. 'He's nice. He has been very good to me.'

'Malachy,' said Brother Declan, 'I have been looking everywhere for you. I wanted to talk about your work tomorrow. And who is this?' he added, eyeing Rory dubiously.

'This is my friend Rory,' said Malachy proudly. 'He's a stone-carver.'

'Ah, yes.' Brother Declan nodded his kind old head. 'Your master is already here, lad, but he is talking to the abbot about the seven stone crosses, so Malachy and I will show you around the abbey while you are waiting for him.'

'He'll no more be able to carve those crosses himself than pigs can fly,' whispered Rory to Malachy, behind his hand. 'You'll see. I'll be the one who does all the fancy work. He's only good for cutting stone – and, of course, for taking all the money in the end.'

'Shhh,' said Malachy warningly, but Brother Declan, who was extremely deaf, only smiled benignly and thought how fortunate it was that Malachy had made a friend. If Rory had not come, there would have been only one other boy of Malachy's age working in the abbey, and that was Colm, the blacksmith's son. Brother Declan sighed as he thought of Colm: a nasty, cunning boy, with a vicious temper. Brother Declan knew that he was a liar and suspected that he was also a thief. No, he would never do as a friend for Malachy, who was delicate and intelligent. This boy Rory, with his honest freckled face and wide grin, would be not only a friend but also a protector for Malachy.

The rain had stopped and it had turned into a beautiful September afternoon. The grey stone abbey had been newly thatched, and its roof shone golden-brown in the clear sunlight. It was such a large building that the cluster of whitewashed cottages around it looked like a flock of chicks around a mother hen. The monks lived in these cottages, mostly two to a cottage; the abbot lived in a slightly larger cottage next to the church. Beyond that was the Scriptorium, where the monks sat to copy out the beautiful books which the abbey owned. Next to the Scriptorium was the workshop where the vellum, the calfskin on which they wrote, was prepared.

'You see, Rory,' explained Malachy, glad of the opportunity to show his knowledge to his friend, 'when the skin is taken from the calves, it's soaked in the river, then scraped clean of hair and flesh. After it has been rinsed again, it's stretched on these frames.'

Rory bent over the frames and touched the skins with his big forefinger. A young monk was scrubbing the skins with a pumice stone, and the places which had already been rubbed were soft and fine.

'What do you use these skins for, then?' he asked.

The young monk looked astonished at his ignorance. 'Why, for the books, of course,' he said.

There was a loud snigger from behind him. Turning around, Rory saw a boy of about thirteen,

Chapter Two

already brawny, with broad shoulders and swelling muscles. His hands were black and he held a heavy hammer, which he swung carelessly from side to side.

'Well, Malachy, you seem to have got yourself an ignorant pig for a friend. Where did you pick him up?'

There was an unmistakable challenge in his black eyes as he stared at them. Rory's freckled face flushed red with anger, and his hands bunched themselves into fists as he took a quick step forward.

'Now then, now then,' Brother Declan intervened. 'Get back to your work, Colm, or I will have to have a word with your father about you. Come on, boys, and I will show you where the hospital and the guest house are. We have many important visitors here, and we never turn away anyone who is ill or in need of food or lodging.'

Brother Declan led the way past the group of whitewashed cottages, past the neatly-tended vegetable rows and the herb garden where Brother David grew all the plants needed for medicines, and through the gatehouse on the south side of the abbey.

'This is the place where one of the seven crosses is going to stand,' he said kindly to Rory. 'I am sure that when you improve at your trade, your master will allow you to help with them.'

Rory tried to look flattered, but the effect was almost spoiled by the wink he bestowed upon Malachy. Brother Declan, however, did not notice, and continued to lead the two boys towards the hospital and the guest house.

Both these buildings were long, low, whitewashed cottages with trim thatched roofs; they were almost identical, but the hospital had an extra room, where an elderly monk stood stirring a green liquid in an iron pot which hung over a smoking turf fire.

'Ah, Brother David,' said Brother Declan genially. 'We have come to visit you on this fine afternoon. You know that Malachy is going to start work with us now, and here is his friend Rory, who is going to help the stonemason with the seven crosses.'

'What are you making, Brother?' asked Malachy with his usual lively curiosity.

Brother David was as small and fat as his friend Brother Declan was tall and thin. His cheeks were pink and he looked as if his herbs had made him very healthy. He always looks so jolly, Malachy thought. No one would ever guess that he spends all his life with sick and dying people.

Brother David smiled as he answered Malachy's question. 'This is comfrey, my son; it makes a useful poultice for putting on wounds.'

'So we're expecting a battle, then?' said Malachy cheekily.

Brother David laughed loud and long, putting down his great iron spoon and seating himself upon his wooden stool in order to enjoy the joke. Rory thought to himself that Malachy was treated rather as a pet by all the Brothers.

Brother Declan, however, did not laugh, and a thoughtful look came over his thin, lined face.

'You may well be right, Malachy,' he said, 'though I hope and pray in God that you are not. Many, many abbeys have been raided in the past few years, and who knows when Kilfenora's turn may come? Anyway, in peace time, as well as in time of battle, the herbs are important to keep us all well and healthy. Tomorrow, Malachy, you will start on the copying;

but first of all, in the morning, I want to show you the herb garden and all the herbs, and explain some of their uses. Brother David and I are not getting any younger, and we need to train someone like you to understand the uses of herbs and to make up the medicines.'

'Yes, Brother,' said Malachy meekly, but Rory could see that he looked impatient under the show of meekness. Rory could understand that. Copying books was Malachy's trade, in the same way that stone-carving was his, and he knew that Malachy did not want anything to distract him from his work.

'Can Malachy show me the place where the books are kept, Brother Declan?' he said aloud. He could see that the sun was low in the sky. Soon it would be too dark to look at the books. The idea of discovering the treasure of Kilfenora was burning strongly inside him, and he could not wait to start on their search.

'Oh, yes,' said Brother Declan, who was now comfortably ensconced on a rush-seated stool beside Brother David's fire, and the two boys left the hospital together.

Malachy was not as confident as Rory that they would find the secret of the treasure in one of the abbey's books; and when he opened the door of the Scriptorium and Rory saw the hundreds of books lining the shelves, he also grew doubtful.

'It would take a man a lifetime to go through all these,' he said in an awed whisper.

'Not really,' said Malachy, trying to sound knowledgeable. 'Wait a minute. Let me think. I'm sure I remember a book about the history of Kilfenora .... Ah, here it is – the Annals of Kilfenora. Could you reach it down for me, Rory? That one there. The plain-looking one.'

Rory reached up and took down the book, handling it carefully and reverentially. It was very thick, its pages curling with age, and it looked very old.

'Well, this starts in the year 900 AD,' said Malachy. 'That's more than three hundred years ago. That should be far enough back.'

He carried the book to the window and began reading, his eye flitting down the page, looking out for anything interesting. There was a long silence, broken only by the sound of Rory's feet pacing up and down the stone-flagged floor.

'Have you found anything yet?' he asked eventually.

'Nothing about treasure,' said Malachy. 'But I've just found something about the herb garden – you remember, Brother Declan showed it to us today. Well, this says "Today Brother Fiachre left us to bring books to the east. He was a good and well-trusted Brother who laboured hard in the herb garden of the abbey."'

'Never mind about the herb garden,' said Rory impatiently. 'Keep looking until you find the word "treasure". I'm sure you'll find some mention of it there. That would be the obvious book to write the secret in, if it's the history of Kilfenora.'

'It might be a bit too obvious,' began Malachy – and then stopped. The door opened and in came Brother Declan.

'Seen everything?' he enquired with a kindly smile. 'I must lock up now. We have many treasures in this Scriptorium, Rory, and we take good care of them. I

17

will meet you tomorrow in the herb garden, Malachy. I don't think you have ever really seen it, have you?'

'Just from the outside, Brother,' said Malachy politely, trying to ignore the huge wink Rory had given him at the word 'treasures'.

The two boys walked down the street in silence and turned in to the little one-roomed house which would be their home for the next few years. They stood for a moment looking out towards the west. The sky was turning grey, but it was still streaked with pink.

'It will be a fine day tomorrow,' said Malachy. 'You'll be able to get on with your stone-cutting, and I'll become wise in the ways of herbs.'

'You would be better off going through that book and finding out where the treasure is hidden,' said Rory bluntly.

Malachy laughed and then yawned. Rory yawned too, and they both climbed into their straw beds. They pulled their blankets over themselves and were soon asleep, dreaming of stone crosses, wonderful books and secret hoards of treasure.

CHAPTER THREE

It was the moon which woke Malachy. Like a great silver plate in the sky, it shone through the open top of the door and filled the little room with almost as much light as the sun. Malachy lay awake, gazing up at it and feeling very happy. He had two new friends and he was going to start work on copying books.

He made a face at the thought of the herb garden. He hated any form of gardening. He hoped he wouldn't have to do any digging. That was something he was hopeless at. I wouldn't mind picking the herbs, he thought, but I want to be a copyist, not a gardener.

He felt restless, a bit too hot, so he threw off his blankets and went over to the door, letting the night air cool his face. Everything was very silent; the sound of a door gently closing was as loud as a slam would have been in daytime. Malachy looked down the street in a puzzled way. Who could be up at this hour of the night? he thought.

Then he saw the dark form which was stealing along the shadowy side of the street. There was an empty space between two houses, where the figure had to emerge from the shadows, and suddenly Malachy could see who it was. It was Colm, the blacksmith's son.

Hastily Malachy drew back into the shadow of his own doorway. What was Colm up to? No good, he was sure of that.

He looked across at Rory, who was snoring peacefully. He decided against trying to wake him; Rory looked like the sort of person who would be hard to wake, and any noise would warn Colm that he had been seen. No, Malachy decided, he would follow Colm himself and see where he was going, and then he would tell Rory all about it in the morning. Quietly he crept over to the fireplace and pulled on his soft leather boots, and then stole out of the door.

Colm was going very slowly, cautiously creeping from house to house and waiting a few minutes in the shadow of each one. Malachy followed with the same caution. He knew he could keep up with Colm; Malachy was a great runner, Colm would never get away from him. On the other hand, if it came to a fight, he knew he would be no match for Colm. I must just keep out of sight and use my brains, he thought.

Colm was going a little more quickly. He had passed all the houses where the monks were living, and only the Scriptorium and the workshops were left before he reached the outer wall of the abbey. Malachy braced himself; Colm will probably start to run as soon as he gets outside the walls, he thought.

But then, to Malachy's astonishment, Colm stopped in front of the Scriptorium. Taking a large key from his pouch, he opened the door and went in.

Malachy crept up and, standing in the shadow of the doorway, peered in. He wondered if Colm was going to try to steal some books, and how he could stop him if he did. Now he was really sorry that he had not tried to wake Rory. He moved back

cautiously. If I'm careful, he thought, I might be able to get back up the street and wake Rory before Colm gets away.

He peeped in at the window once more and then stopped, feeling rather puzzled. The walls of the Scriptorium were lined with shelves, and each shelf was filled with precious books; gold, purple and blue gleamed from their covers. But Colm had not touched any of these. He had gone straight to the small shelves at the back of the Scriptorium and had picked out the very same book which Malachy himself had been reading just a few hours before.

Malachy stared at him in amazement. That book was of little value to anyone except the monks of

Kilfenora. What on earth is Colm doing? he wondered – and then a stifled laugh escaped him. He knew it was stupid to make a sound, but he could not help it: he could see quite clearly, by the light of the moon, that Colm was holding the book upside down and peering at it earnestly, as if determined to extract a meaning from it.

The night was silent, and that half-stifled sound was enough to tell Colm that he was being watched. He dropped the Annals of Kilfenora on the ground and bounded to the door. He grabbed Malachy by the hood of his tunic, and Malachy knew that only one thing could save him.

'Rory!' he shouted. 'Rory, help me!'

For a moment Colm hesitated – and then, to Malachy's intense relief, the door of the large house between the Scriptorium and the church opened and the tall figure of the abbot came out.

'What is going on here?' he asked with quiet authority. 'Colm, let go of Malachy instantly. Now, both of you, tell me what this is all about.'

Colm said nothing, just looked sullenly at the ground. Malachy made a quick decision that the truth – though perhaps not all of the truth – was the best policy, so he spoke quickly, before Colm had a chance to tell any lie.

'I couldn't sleep, Father,' he said. 'I was too hot. I got out of bed and went to the door to cool myself down. While I was standing there I saw Colm go down the street and into the Scriptorium. I followed him to see what he was doing, and then he came out and caught hold of me, and I yelled for Rory to come and save me because I thought Colm was going to kill me.' And where *is* Rory? he thought indignantly. Talk about heavy sleeping! I could be dead by now!

'Now, Malachy, don't exaggerate,' said the abbot sharply. 'I am sure that Colm was not going to kill you. But what *were* you doing in the Scriptorium in the middle of the night, Colm?'

'He's telling lies, Father,' said Colm, who by then had had time to think of a story. 'He was the one who went into the Scriptorium. I just followed him to see what he was doing, and then he tried to run away.'

The abbot looked at him doubtfully, and then walked forward and took the key out of the door.

'Now I know that you are the one who is telling lies, Colm,' he said severely. 'This is my own key, and I brought it to your father yesterday to have the top of it repaired. I can see the damaged bit quite clearly. You stole it from your father's workshop, and I think you tried to steal from the Scriptorium. Now what have you to say for yourself?'

Colm said nothing. The abbot frowned and turned to Malachy. 'Lock the door, Malachy,' he said. 'Make sure that all the books are in their proper places, and then go back to your house. I want to talk to Colm.'

'Yes, Father,' said Malachy meekly. He went into the Scriptorium, picked up the Annals of Kilfenora, and dragged over a small stool so that he could put it back on the shelf. Then he turned and looked out. The abbot and Colm had moved a little distance away, and neither was looking at him, so he quickly slipped the book into his pouch and rearranged the others on the shelf so that no gap remained. Carefully he locked the door and handed the key to the abbot. Then he set off running down the street to the house which he shared with Rory.

Once inside the house, he waited patiently until the abbot and Colm were both safely back in their houses. Then, trembling with excitement, he tugged at Rory's arm.

'Wake up, Rory!' he said urgently. 'Wait until you hear what happened tonight!'

Rory yawned, sat up, rubbed the sleep from his eyes, and then sank back down again.

'Oh, wake up,' said Malachy impatiently. 'It was a good job that the abbot rescued me. Colm could have killed me and buried my body before you woke up.'

At that Rory sat bolt upright, all traces of sleep gone from him, and Malachy laughed happily. He loved to tell a story to an audience, and this was a dramatic story that he had to tell.

'So the only question is,' he finished, 'does Colm know anything about the treasure of Kilfenora, or did he just overhear what we were saying and go to find the same book when everyone was asleep? The thing that puzzles me, though, is that he can't read, so how could he hope to find anything out by just looking at the book?'

'Perhaps he thought there might be something like a map inside the book, or even a plan,' said Rory thoughtfully. 'I was thinking of something like that myself.'

'That's an idea,' said Malachy. Holding the book carefully so that the firelight fell on the creamy-brown leaves, he slowly turned the pages over, one by one, until he reached the end.

'No,' he said, looking up into Rory's eager face. 'No trace of a map or anything like that. It's quite a dull book, really. It seems to be mostly about the names of visitors and the names of monks who died and the

24

names of monks who travelled to the east, like Brother Fiachre who made the herb garden. There are two quite exciting bits about when the abbey was raided and burnt down and then built up again.'

'And that's all?'

'Well, I'll go through it again. I'm a quick reader. It won't take me too long.'

'I'll heat up some milk for a drink while you're reading,' said Rory.

Once again Malachy skimmed through the pages. 'I wish I knew what exactly I'm looking for,' he said, when he was about halfway through. 'I'm sure you were right when you said it would probably be written in the form of a puzzle, but I can't think what to look for – except something about burying jars or chests, or perhaps something about a secret.'

Rory grunted, but did not seem to have any more ideas. Malachy returned to his reading, but by the time Rory had poured the milk into two wooden goblets he had put the book down in despair.

'It's no good,' he said. 'I can't find anything about the treasure.'

'Don't give up hope,' said Rory. 'That's not the only book. You can look through the others from time to time; there's no rush. Don't let this spoil everything for us. We're going to have a great time. I'm looking forward to carving the stone crosses, and you're looking forward to writing your books. We'll just forget about tonight.'

Malachy said nothing. He looked downcast, and Rory tried to distract him.

'Why do the monks spend so much time copying books?' he asked.

Malachy roused himself a little. 'Well, the books get worn out by so much handling,' he said. 'Of course, they sell some of the copies, especially out in the east, to the great libraries in places like Constantinople .... Anyway, tell me about the stone crosses. We've only had wooden ones before. There are seven of them: three around the church and four on the boundaries of the abbey enclosure. They've been there for a long time, Brother Declan was telling me, and all the wood is getting rotten.'

'Well, that won't happen with the stone crosses,' said Rory confidently. 'They'll last a thousand years.'

'What are you going to carve on them?' enquired Malachy.

'I don't really know,' said Rory. 'My master has some patterns, and usually I copy something from that – probably Jesus or one of the saints, and then some spirals or something underneath. What are you looking so excited about?'

'I've just had a great idea. There are some wonderful pictures and patterns in the books in the Scriptorium. While I'm copying the books I can copy some of them onto a piece of vellum, one of the small scrap pieces, and then you can carve them onto the crosses. The crosses of Kilfenora will be the most famous in the whole country by the time we're finished with them!'

'And by the time you've gone through all the books in the Scriptorium, you will have found the secret of the treasure,' said Rory. He tossed his empty goblet in the air and caught it neatly as it came down. 'And you'll be the best maker of books in Ireland, and I'll be the most famous stone-carver.'

They both went to the door and looked out. The brilliant moonshine lit up the whole street, the little cottages and the big church.

'Let's go to bed,' said Malachy. 'It will be a lovely day tomorrow.'

CHAPTER FOUR

The next day was indeed a lovely one. There was a slight frost in the early morning but this soon cleared to a beautiful fine day. Rory set to work with his master, the mason, and Malachy joined Brother David and Brother Declan in the herb garden.

The herb garden was a small, neat enclosure quite near to Malachy's and Rory's house. It had high hedges all around it, to protect it from the strong winds that blew in from the sea, and inside these hedges it was warm and sheltered. Several bees were buzzing around and sucking nectar from the few flowers which were still left on the herbs.

'You see, Malachy,' explained Brother Declan, 'the hedges are important because the plants grow better when they are sheltered and the bees like it better, too. They hate strong winds. Bees are very important to us, because without honey we would have nothing to sweeten our food.'

'What are these hedges for?' asked Malachy, pointing to the little hedges between the herbs.

'These are made from a plant called box, and they make a little box around each different herb.'

'I like these best,' observed Malachy thoughtfully.

Someone had gone to a lot of trouble when they planted these hedges of box, he thought to himself. The hedges were not just planted in lines, making rectangles and squares, but twisted and wound in and out, crossing and crisscrossing.

'I know,' he said aloud, 'it's like the pattern in the margin of some of the books which you've shown me.'

Brother Declan's face lit up with pride. 'Clever boy,' he said. 'These hedges are supposed to be hundreds of years old, and I have heard it said that they were copied from some book. There is no doubt that it is very like the patterns that we see in many of our books.'

'Now this herb here is comfrey, Malachy,' said Brother David. 'This is the herb for wounds and sores in man, and it also makes a drink to help the healing. And this is sage for sore throats, and this is rosemary for rheumatism, and this is skullcap for ...'

'That skullcap herb has a different pattern of hedge around it,' interrupted Malachy.

Brother David stared and then laughed. 'Well, do you know, I have been picking herbs in this garden for thirty years and I have never noticed that before.'

'The boy is right, though, you know,' mused Brother Declan, staring with the professional eye of a copyist at the intricate pattern of hedging around the skull-shaped purple flowers.

'I have never seen a pattern like that before,' he added decisively, after a few more minutes of thought, 'and I know every book in the library. That pattern certainly does not come from any book in Kilfenora.'

Brother David went on explaining the uses of every herb, but Malachy's lively mind became bored and he began to wonder about the different pattern around that one herb. Perhaps the monk who was planting the hedges had got tired by the time he came to the skullcap bed and decided to change patterns. It did seem odd, though, to use one pattern around nineteen herbs and then change it for the twentieth. Perhaps there was some other reason for the strange pattern. With the toe of his boot Malachy drew the design on the dry, dusty earth of the path.

'Brother Declan,' he said abruptly and impatiently, 'I don't think that I will ever be able to remember all that Brother David is telling me. Have you got a book where it's all written down? I learn much better by reading things than by listening to people telling me things.'

'Remember your manners, Malachy,' said Brother Declan warningly, but Brother David was not offended.

'You book-men are all the same,' he laughed. 'You set him to work on that old Herbal, Brother Declan. He can copy it out; it's very worn and old and will soon fall to pieces. As he is copying it he will learn about the herbs. But don't forget about the real plants, lad,' he added, putting a kindly arm around Malachy's shoulders. 'When you have copied out the writing and finished the drawing, come out here to the herb garden and smell and touch the real plants.'

Malachy, who was a little ashamed of his rudeness, smiled his best smile at the gentle old man.

'I'll do even better, Brother David,' he said. 'When I finish copying the writing I'll come outside here and I'll paint a picture of each herb in your herb garden. That way I'll be able to match the colours and the shapes exactly.'

So that afternoon Malachy began his first task at the monastery. The Herbal was arranged in alphabetical order, so Malachy started with '*Achillea Millefolium*', yarrow. With a very fine paintbrush made from the hairs of a squirrel's tail, Malachy stroked a perfect triangular capital A; around it, lightly and delicately, he painted an exact copy of the feathery leaves of the yarrow. Only when the last tiny stroke was completed did he draw his breath and lay down his brush.

As he sat waiting for his masterpiece to dry, Malachy thought once again about the strange pattern in the herb garden. He turned over the pages of the old Herbal until he came to 'S'. '*Scutellaria lateriflora*,' skullcap, he read; 'most potent and useful for headaches and for rheumatism.' There were no patterns on this page, nor on any of the pages of the Herbal. In fact, it was quite a plain book. Malachy made up his mind that he was going to make a copy of such rich and rare beauty that it would far excel the original. Delicately he touched the smooth, soft surface of the new vellum pages and admired the way the rich blue-black of the letter 'A' stood out against the ivory whiteness of the page. He would copy that pattern of the box hedges down the side of each page, he decided, and instead of gold he would use a dark, shining green. And when he came to the page for skullcap, he would change the pattern; and hundreds of years later, when the herb garden of Kilfenora Abbey no longer existed, people would wonder why the pattern on that particular page had been changed.

As Malachy sat there, smiling to himself and dreaming of the day when he would have finished the last page, '*Viola Odorata*,' he heard a great commotion outside. Going to the door of the Scriptorium, he met the blacksmith's son.

'What's happening, Colm?' he asked.

'Oh, some old monk who has been out in the east has come to stay in the guest house. He has chests full of old books which he's brought back across the sea for the library at Kilfenora. The Abbot is making a great fuss and all the rest of the Brothers are flying around in circles. I suppose you'll be running up there to have a peep, too.'

'Certainly not,' said Malachy with great dignity. 'I have my work to do, and you would be better advised to get on with your own work and not come disturbing me.'

He turned on his heel and walked back inside. If he had seen the look of black hatred which Colm cast in his direction, he might have been very disturbed indeed.

CHAPTER FIVE

When Malachy came into the Scriptorium early next morning, he saw that he was not the first to arrive. Seated at the table under the window was a very old monk, his skin dried and browned by living in sunny places and his hair as white as snow.

'Good morning,' he said, in a voice which was weak and thin. 'I am Brother Mark, and you must be Malachy.'

Malachy bowed politely, then drew near and peered over Brother Mark's shoulder.

'What a beautiful book,' he gasped.

It was, indeed, a beautiful book. Its cover was made from vellum dyed a rich purple; the letters on it were made from gold; the borders of the covers were filled with exquisite flowers. Malachy recognised some of the flowers – the early spring marsh orchids and the lady's-tress orchids which flowered in the damp meadows around Drumshee.

'I've painted flowers like these,' he said shyly. 'They grow around here.'

The old monk smiled. 'Ah,' he said, 'you have a quick eye. This book is the Psalter of King David. It was made here in Kilfenora a long time ago, and from here it was taken out to the east. It must be hundreds of years old and it is very precious. While strength remains to me I am going to try to make a copy of it, and when I die, you must carry on my work. I have been looking at the first page of the Herbal which you

34

are doing, and it is exquisite work. You show wonderful promise. In the time that is left to me I will try to show you all that I have learned, here in Ireland and abroad in cities like Constantinople. But first, you must meet my friend.'

From the depths of his lap, buried in the folds of his gown, the old man lifted something up. Again Malachy gasped in astonishment. It was not a book this time, but a cat. Malachy had always loved cats. Even the half-wild cats around the farmyard had been petted and spoiled and given milk by him, but this cat was something completely different. It had fur like cream silk, a long triangular face with a dark brown mask, and bright blue eyes. His whole heart went out to the beautiful creature. Very gently he ran his hand along the slim body, which arched with pleasure at his touch, and felt with wonder the strangely kinked tail.

'This is Xanadu,' said the old man proudly. 'You spell it with an X, although it sounds as if it should be a Z. I bought him from a sailor in Constantinople. The sailor said that he found him, but I suspect that he was stolen from Siam, because these cats are the royal cats of Siam. I have heard it said that they live on silk cushions in royal palaces, but Xanadu is happy in a monk's cell. He is my faithful friend.'

Xanadu did look royal. His small well-shaped head was held high, and his eyes gazed directly at Malachy with all the assurance of a young prince. It seemed that Xanadu liked what he saw, because with one lithe spring he leaped from the old man's lap on to Malachy's shoulders and coiled himself around the boy's neck, purring loudly.

'Well,' said Brother Mark with astonishment, 'I have never seen him do that to anyone except me. He has chosen you for his second friend, and you must be proud of that. If anything happens to me, you must promise me to love and care for him, and he will repay you with the precious gift of his love.'

Glowing with pleasure, Malachy sat down at his table, trying not to disturb the cat. He need not have worried: Xanadu remained firmly attached to him, settling down like a warm silk scarf around Malachy's neck as he picked up his brush and began, slowly and carefully, to outline the first letter of the next page of the Herbal. '*Aloe Vera*,' he read; 'take one leaf and break it, and apply to burns or sore skin.'

When will I get to skullcap? he wondered impatiently. But he knew that beautiful work could not be hurried. Each page had to be as perfect as possible and was offered up as a prayer to God. He dipped his fine brush into the small pot of green colour and, with a slow and steady hand, began to trace the knotwork pattern down the side of the page.

Several hours went by as the two scribes, old and young, worked quietly side by side. What lovely peace there is in a monastery, thought Malachy. That was one of the things that he had hated at the farm: there always seemed to be such a lot of shouting and disturbances and things going wrong.

'*Alchemilla mollis*,' he wrote in his elegant script. This was the plant called Our Lady's Mantle, so he planned the page carefully, with a picture of Our Lady, the mother of God, in the centre of the page and the writing arranged around it. He drew a delicate oval for the face, outlined a gentle mouth, and then began work on the eyes. They would be a deep blue,

he decided, blue as the gentians on the Burren, and Our Lady's hair would be a shining black under the blue folds of her veil.

He worked on happily, and when he eventually laid his brush down, he cared nothing for the stiff coldness of his fingers nor for his cramped muscles, because he knew, quite simply, that it was the best work that he had ever done.

He lifted his head and realised that Brother Mark and the cat had gone, and that the sun was setting, but he was not alone. There in front of him was the living image of the picture that he had painted. With a start of surprise, Malachy understood why the picture of Our Lady looked so real. He had painted a portrait of Rory's sister, Mary.

'Malachy,' she was saying, 'Malachy, are you coming? I've made supper for you and Rory. Rory is already sitting there, starving hungry. He has chiselled out three stone bowls and he says that if he doesn't get fed soon, he will eat the bowls.'

Malachy laughed and got to his feet. He went quickly over to the door, not wanting Mary to see the picture which was so astonishingly like her. He carefully locked the door and took the big key over to Brother Declan's house. Outside his house, Brother Declan stood talking to Brother Mark.

'I've locked the door, Brother Declan,' Malachy explained, 'because Brother Mark has left his book inside.'

'Quite right, too,' said Brother Mark approvingly. 'That book is beyond all price. Nothing must happen to it. There are evil men who would give their lives to possess it.'

'Mary,' called Malachy, 'come and meet Xanadu, the royal cat of Siam.'

'Royal?' said a rough voice behind him. 'Why is it royal? Is that cat worth any money ?'

Malachy turned around and saw the dirty figure of the blacksmith's boy.

'Colm,' he said loftily, 'I wonder why you are always listening to other people's conversations. It must be because you never have anything worthwhile to say yourself.'

Mary giggled, and then they both forgot Colm as they stood worshipping the beautiful cat. Xanadu refused to leave his master's arms this time, but he did allow Mary to rub gently under his chin and to feel the strange kink at the end of his tail.

'There is an old story,' said Brother Mark, pleased at their interest, 'that a Siamese princess slipped her precious rings over the tail of her cat before she went to bathe in the river, and the faithful cat was so worried that the rings might be lost that he kinked the end of his tail so that none of them could slide off. Ever since then, all Siamese cats have had kinked tails.'

Mary smiled with delight at the story and Malachy, watching her, thought how much he would like to buy her a precious ring. If I could sell something at the fair at Noughal, he thought, I might be able to buy her a present.

'Come on,' he said aloud, 'we had better get back before Rory starts eating his bowls.'

'Wait a moment,' said Brother Mark suddenly. 'I want to show you something, Malachy. You come too, Mary; it will only take a moment.'

He led the boy and girl into the abbey church, up the aisle and into the chancel, and stopped beside a large limestone slab set in the floor.

'This is the tomb of St Fachtnan,' he said quietly. 'Look closely at it and tell me what you see.'

Malachy bent over the slab and peered intently at it. The slab had been carved away so that the figure on it stood out from the surface. It was a man, dressed in a loose tunic and wearing a small skullcap. The man's neck was long and looked as if it were encased in some form of collar, his eyes were looking down, and his slender fingers held a flat object. A sudden idea came to Malachy and he looked up in excitement.

'Is it a book?' he asked. 'Is he holding a book, perhaps? Could it be that book which you're copying?'

'No one knows,' said the old man, leaning over and touching the figure of St Fachtnan reverentially. 'All I know is that several old manuscripts mention the book of St Fachtnan. So who knows? It is a fact that the Psalter is very old, and certainly it came from Kilfenora Abbey. That is written on it. Now go with Mary and have your meal, and tomorrow you can look at the book again.'

Pale with excitement, Malachy followed Mary down the street. It was only as they were going through the door of the house that it occurred to him to wonder whether Colm had overheard the conversation about this most precious book.

CHAPTER SIX

Two years went by – two long quiet years, during which Malachy finished his Herbal and Rory completed six of the crosses of Kilfenora and began work on the seventh. Malachy and Rory were still the best of friends. Every Sunday morning, Malachy went with Rory to the little farmhouse on the Burren and had his Sunday meal with Rory's family; and often on Sunday afternoons, or after work was finished, Malachy took Rory and Mary to Drumshee.

Nobody lived there now. The thatch on the house had rotted and the roof timbers were collapsing, but they did not bother too much about the house; they were too interested in the souterrain, the underground room in the middle of the fort. On wet Sunday afternoons they lit a fire in there, and gradually they made it comfortable, bringing in slabs of stone and piles of bracken to sit on and placing candles in the little ledges in the stone walls. They had a little iron pot which Mary's mother had found to be useless with her large family, and Rory made a shelf, on one of the walls, where they could keep dried herbs and three wooden cups. On fine Sundays they roamed all around the farm, finding old broken branches of hawthorn and ash and stacking them in the corner of the underground chamber, so that they always had a good supply of wood. And all this time Malachy found that he was becoming more and more in love with Mary.

In the meantime, Brother Mark was still working slowly and painfully upon the Psalter of King David. Xanadu, the royal cat of Siam, grew sleek and rounded upon the diet of fish caught for him by Rory and Malachy. Xanadu tolerated Mary and condescended to drink some of the cream which she often brought for him, but he turned and walked away with his tail held high in the air whenever Rory approached him, and he arched his back and spat whenever he saw Colm. The only people who really existed for him were Brother Mark and Malachy, and these two he loved with all his strange little oriental heart.

It was September again, but a September quite unlike that golden month when Rory and Malachy had joined the monastery at Kilfenora. This was a wet and stormy September. Day after day, the strong southwesterly winds blew and the rain swept through the village in sudden torrential waves. The herb garden lay sodden in heaps of green and brown foliage, and the monks, going about their daily business, scurried down the main street with hoods pulled almost over their eyes and their backs bent against the fierce onslaught of the wind.

Rory was the only one who seemed to take no notice of the weather. He was now sixteen years old, a strong, brawny lad. Malachy had also grown during the last two years, but next to Rory he still appeared small and slight.

It was a Saturday, and Rory was out in a field about two hundred yards west of the abbey church, helping the master mason to select a place for the seventh cross. The High Cross was going to be the largest and most magnificent which they had done yet. It was sixteen feet high, carved from one solid slab of limestone, and Rory planned that it would have the finest carvings of all. Already Malachy had been hard at work copying designs from books in the library on

to odd pieces of vellum. Tonight Mary was coming to cook them a special supper, and then all three of them were going to work on the final design for the High Cross.

At six in the evening, therefore, Rory stuck his wet tousled head into the studious, quiet atmosphere of the Scriptorium. 'Are you coming, Malachy?' he enquired in a voice which he intended to be soft and gentle, but which struck the two scribes like a raw explosion of sound. They both looked up reluctantly, shivering slightly as the cold, damp air from outside penetrated their cosy little cell. Malachy got slowly to his feet, his eyes still on the beautiful flowing pattern which he had just created down the margin of the page. With an absent-minded air he cleaned the brush he had been using.

'Are you going back to the guest house now, Brother?' he enquired.

Brother Mark shook his head. 'No, my son,' he said. 'I want to finish this page tonight. Put some more turf on for me before you leave. I will have a little sleep by the fire for an hour and then I will continue. Old men are like cats; they like a little nap from time to time, but they don't need a long night's sleep.'

Malachy did as he was bid, but he glanced at the old man in a worried way. Brother Mark had always looked old, but now he looked almost transparent. The hand that stroked Xanadu was the same parchment colour as the soft silky fur on the cat's back. It's just willpower which is keeping him alive, thought Malachy; the strength of his will to finish copying the sacred Psalter of King David. He gazed at the old man with pity. He remembered a phrase from the Gospel of St Mark which he had been copying a few days before: *the spirit is willing, but the flesh is weak.*

This Mark was indeed willing, but he was very weak. His copy of the Psalter of King David was as exquisite as the original, but it was proceeding at a painfully slow pace.

Malachy went sadly out of the door, pulling his rough cloak around him. Outside in the street the wind made him gasp and robbed him of his breath for an instant.

On the corner of the street, near to the blacksmith's shop, Colm stood talking to a strange man with a great head of bushy hair and a large black moustache. Malachy wondered briefly who the man was, but it was too cold and too wet for even Malachy to feel curious. So he and Rory struggled on until they reached their little house, where a welcoming light glowed from the window.

Inside everything was bright and cheerful. The table was laid with the stone bowls and with three goblets of carved applewood, which had been given to them by one of the Brothers. The turf fire was burning brightly and above it, hanging from the iron crane, was a steaming black pot.

'That smells nice,' said Malachy, banishing from his mind the sad picture of Brother Mark toiling away at a task which seemed to have no end.

'I've cooked those birds which Rory got with his sling,' said Mary, ladling out the rich brown stew from the pot.

'Looks lovely!' said Rory.

'Looks lovely,' agreed Malachy, but he was thinking less of the food than of the lovely picture which Mary made, with her pink cheeks and blue eyes and damp curls.

That evening the three friends worked hard at the design for the seventh cross. Malachy had already decided that he wanted a copy of the strange pattern of the box hedges around the skullcap herb to be carved at the bottom of the west face of the cross. The abbot wanted the top of the east face to show the Crucifixion. First Malachy sketched a crucified Christ with a crown of thorns, but then he changed his mind and drew within the cross shape a picture of the risen Christ, with a long tunic and a halo around his head.

'You see,' he explained, 'this side of the cross will face the east, so it will symbolise the rising of Jesus from the dead.'

While Malachy was doing this, Mary was arranging the patterns which he had brought home into blocks to be carved on the stem of the cross, and Rory was studying their intricacies with a professional eye.

'Some of these will be rather difficult to do,' he remarked, 'but I think I can manage. I've got much better than I was two years ago. Even my miserly old master admits that I'm worth more money now. He even offered to increase my pay today.'

'You haven't found the treasure of Kilfenora yet, then,' observed Mary slyly.

'That was probably just some old story,' said Malachy regretfully. 'I've looked though all the books in the library, and none of them seem to have a treasure map in them or anything of the sort.'

'Perhaps the book might have been taken away from Kilfenora. After all, the book which Brother

Mark is copying was originally written in Kilfenora and then taken away to the east,' said Rory.

'Well, never mind,' said Mary cheerfully. 'If you work hard at your carving you may end up with lots of money anyway, and Malachy is going to be a monk so he shouldn't want any money.'

Malachy said nothing, but he felt a hot flush come over his cheeks. He was fourteen years old, and soon it would be time for him to decide whether he did really want to be a monk. Life was not so easy as it had been when he was eleven or twelve, he decided. He looked across at Mary, busily fitting the pieces of pattern together, and thought how nice it would be to marry her and have a little house to live in, just like this one.

He sighed. He was no longer sure that he wanted to be a monk, but he did not know how he could support a wife. One thing was certain: he would never be a farmer. But what else could he do? He sighed even more heavily, and the wind outside seemed to echo his sigh, as a strong gust rattled against the shutters and moaned in the chimney.

Or *was* it the wind? Malachy lifted his head and listened intently. There it was again: a harsh wailing sound. Was it the wind, or was it a banshee? Malachy felt the hair on the back of his neck stand up. Across the table Mary's eyes were shocked, wide circles of blue.

'What in thunder was that?' whispered Rory. They all three listened intently. Again and again the strange high shrieking sound came. Rory strode across to the door, flung the two halves open and stared out into the darkness.

'In the name of God, who are you and what do you want?' he demanded. There was no answer, but a small, creamy shape catapulted into the little house. There stood Xanadu, his wet fur standing up in sharp hackles and those strange wailing sounds coming from his open mouth.

'Xanadu, what is the matter?' cried Mary in great distress. 'Oh, Malachy, is he injured?'

Malachy picked up the cat and felt him all over. 'He's not hurt in any way,' he said, 'but there is something badly wrong. I've never seen him leave Brother Mark before. And he's shaking all over.'

He went to the door of the house, still holding the trembling body of the little cat close to his chest, and looked down the dark village street. They had been working late. We must take Mary home or her father will be worried, he thought, his mind moving with an unaccustomed slowness. But as he looked around he could see that they were not the only ones still awake. Through the window of the Scriptorium there showed a light, and as Malachy and Rory gazed down the street a shadow moved between the candle and the window. It was the shadow of a burly, big man with wide shoulders and a shock of unruly hair. It definitely was not Brother Mark.

Malachy's eyes met Rory's, and simultaneously they both thought of the man with whom Colm had been speaking that afternoon.

'I knew he was up to mischief,' whispered Rory. 'He keeps disappearing these days. His father is always looking for him.'

'Hold Xanadu, Mary,' said Malachy in a low voice. 'We must see what has happened to Brother Mark.'

Moving quietly, the two of them rapidly crossed the open space of ground to the village street. As they came around the corner of Brother Declan's house, which stood opposite the Scriptorium, Malachy placed a warning hand upon Rory's arm and they both stopped in the deep shadow of the wall. They were not alone. The village street was full of men, all moving quietly, dressed in dark cloaks. They seemed like shadows moving down the dark street, but here and there the light from the slender new moon caught the blade of a weapon. The abbey was going to be attacked.

'Wait here,' whispered Malachy. 'Watch the Scriptorium and see that no harm comes to Brother Mark. I'm going to toll the abbey bell. All the men from miles around know that the bell is the signal for danger, and they will all come to save the abbey.'

Quickly and lightly, he slipped around the back of the house and ran down the lane. He pulled open the heavy door of the bell-tower and climbed to the top of the ladder. With all his strength he pulled on the bell-rope, and the great bell rang out with a deafening clamour over the countryside.

A few minutes before, Malachy had been very conscious of the howling of the wind; but the heavy tolling of the bell blotted out all other sounds. Again and again he swung on the heavy ropes, and again and again the deafening sound rang out, until Malachy began to feel sick and dizzy. He let go of the rope and listened.

At first he could hear nothing because the noise of the bell still echoed in his ears, but gradually other sounds began to pierce his numbed brain.

He climbed back down the ladder. Slipping out of the door, he could hear angry shouts, and he saw that the street was full of men carrying weapons. The raiders had swords and knives, but the defenders had equally deadly weapons: their sickles, their pickaxes, their spades, and the heavy rocks which littered the fields.

The street was no longer dark, as the pitch torches were held aloft, and this time Malachy did not bother to go by the back lanes; he ran straight down the main village street, dodging the warring figures, until he reached the Scriptorium.

To his relief, Mary, with Xanadu in her arms, was there next to Rory, bending over the figure of Brother Mark. But Malachy's relief soon turned to a cold fear. One glance at the old monk was enough: the heavy eyelids were shut, the parchment skin was a dead white and the thin lips were blue. One hand still clutched the ancient Psalter of King David, but the other was pressed over his heart and he moaned gently. Malachy gazed at him in an agony of pity and terror.

Brother Mark opened his eyes. 'Take the book,' he whispered painfully. 'Take the book and hide it. Do not come back to Kilfenora until all is safe. That book is the greatest treasure in the whole kingdom. Men will plunder and kill for this book. Take it and keep it safe.'

With all his remaining strength, he lifted the book and thrust it at Malachy. Then his head fell forward and his whole body slumped across the table. Malachy picked up the heavy hand and felt for the pulse, but even before his fingers touched the wrist he knew what he would find. Brother Mark was dead.

CHAPTER SEVEN

Five minutes later, Malachy, carrying Xanadu and with the precious book tucked into the pocket of his cloak, was running through the back lanes of Kilfenora once more. Behind him came Rory and Mary, doing their best to keep up.

This time, however, Malachy did not turn up towards the abbey. Without hesitating, he took the path across the fields, towards Drumshee. 'Take the book,' Brother Mark had said, 'take it and keep it safe'; and Malachy had immediately known where he could go to keep the book and them all safe. On he ran, sure-footed and fast, dodging rocks and leaping over stones, until he realised that he could no longer hear Rory puffing and panting behind him.

I must have outrun them, he thought. He slowed up, and then began to feel rather anxious. He could see nothing but the flames of the torches in the village street in the distance. The rain still fell, and there was an ominous growl of thunder. Xanadu began shivering again. The little cat hated thunder and always crawled under Brother Mark's chair when there was a thunderstorm.

At that moment the whole sky was lit up with an enormous sheet of blue lightning. In its glare, Malachy could see the figure of Mary, wrapped in her brown cloak, running as fast as she could along the path; and behind her was, not Rory, but a burly man with a shock of unruly hair. It was the man whom

51

they had seen in the Scriptorium, the man who had been talking with Colm, and in a sudden flash of comprehension Malachy understood that this man had come to steal the precious book, the Psalter of King David.

He watched the scene in an agony of fear. He did not know what had become of Rory, but he knew that he himself was not strong enough to tackle a man like that without help. The only chance was for him to divert the fellow. No matter how valuable the book might be, it was of little account to Malachy compared to Mary's safety.

He got to his feet with a great cry. The man stopped, startled. At that moment, clearly outlined in the blue-white light, another figure rose up from behind the hedge; a huge boulder was lifted high and crashed down on top of the unruly hair, and the man fell to the ground like a pole-axed bullock.

'Well, that should hold him for an hour or so,' remarked Rory. 'Don't worry, Mary, he's not dead, but he'll have a headache in the morning.'

The thunder rumbled again. A few seconds later, when the next flash of lightning came, they looked anxiously back towards the village. The lightning did not last long, but it was long enough for them to make sure that there were no other pursuers.

'I think that he and Colm are the only ones who know about the book,' said Malachy in a low voice. 'The rest of the party are probably just ordinary raiders trying to steal from the abbey. But let's go as fast as we can, in case I'm wrong. We'll make for Drumshee. No one will find us in that underground chamber. It's all right, Xanadu,' he added, stroking the little cat gently. 'The storm is passing away now, and we'll soon have you dry and warm.'

Though there did not appear to be any more pursuers, the three still ran as fast as they could, stopping occasionally to draw breath and to listen for anyone coming after them. There was no sound behind them, however; only the howling of the wind and the pattering of the rain on the rocks. The rain was falling in great sheets and the westerly wind was strong at their backs, making it easy to run but driving the rain through their heavy woollen cloaks and soaking them to the skin. I wonder what's happening at the abbey, thought Malachy, as he neatly jumped a large marshy piece of ground. I hope Brother Declan and Brother David are safe. His mind slid away from the thought of Brother Mark's body slumped over the table.

He stopped to wait for Mary and Rory. They had been running and walking and running again for about half an hour, and Malachy could see that Mary was tiring.

'Nearly there,' he said cheerfully. 'We can walk now. We'll be at Drumshee once we cross this field.'

There were cows in the big meadow, he noticed, and also in the rough field. Some of his kin must have taken over the farm; the land was poor and waterlogged, but it would be good winter grazing for some prosperous farmer. Malachy did not care who had it. He was certain that he himself never wanted to farm.

They crossed the field without talking, and waited in the shadow of the hedge until they were sure that no one was about.

'We'll keep beside the hedge when we go up the Togher field,' he said in a low voice. 'In these times, it's hard to know who is a friend and who is an enemy, so it would be best not to be seen.'

The moon had gone behind the clouds, so they made their way safely to the entrance of the underground chamber. They squeezed past the blackthorn and edged their way down the pitch-dark passageway, feeling the walls on either side of them, until they reached the chamber itself. Still holding Xanadu, Malachy felt around until he found the flint and tinder box.

'Here, Rory,' he said. 'Strike a light for us and we'll soon get a fire going.'

In a few minutes Rory managed to get the tinder to burn, and Mary set a candle on top of the flagstone which they used for a table. The underground chamber had been very well built, and it was warm and dry after the wild storm outside. Malachy knew that they would have to get a fire going quickly, though. Mary's lips were blue, and Xanadu was shivering with fright and cold.

'Thank goodness we gathered so much dry wood the last time we were here,' he said aloud. 'Mary, you hold Xanadu; Rory, you light the fire; and I'll go out to the well and get some water. I can see in the dark better than you two. A nice hot drink of camomile will help us all to feel more comfortable.'

Mary smiled. Malachy was being the man in charge, as usual. He was not just clever, she thought admiringly; there were many clever people at the abbey, but Malachy was the most practical and quick-thinking of them all. He always knew exactly what to do and usually found someone to do it for him. I'm sure he'll end up as the Abbot, she thought – and surprised herself by feeling rather sad that he was going to be a monk. She blushed a little at her thoughts, and Malachy, coming in with the pot of water, smiled happily to see her looking less pale.

'Here we are,' he said triumphantly, holding up a fat young hare in his other hand. 'Look at what I have. Do you remember that you set a snare last Sunday, Rory? Well, we forgot to look on our way home, and now – what luck! We may be days here – it depends on how long the fighting lasts – but at least we won't go hungry.'

'Lucky that we kept the old knife you found here,' said Rory cheerfully, rising from his seat. 'I could just do with some roast hare. It seems ages since supper.'

Mary laughed and began to feel more cheerful herself. Rory would always be hungry, she thought affectionately, as she watched him expertly cleaning the hare. And he would always live for the moment. She knew by looking at him that no worries about the future were troubling his mind. Malachy was also a little like that. He did what needed to be done, as quickly and efficiently as possible, and then put it out of his head. He wasn't like her, always worrying about the future.

The hare, roasted in strips on the tip of Malachy's knife, tasted delicious. Xanadu had some of it as well, but he wasn't his usual hungry self. He kept looking around the cave in a bewildered way, as if searching for Brother Mark; and once he reached up and tapped Malachy on the face with his paw, and then gave a piercing miaow, as if asking to be brought back to his beloved master. Malachy felt a lump grow in his throat. He was doing his best to avoid thinking of

Brother Mark, and the cat was not making matters much better. He hastily swallowed some of the fragrant camomile drink and started to talk.

'Now then,' he said authoritatively, 'we must plan for tomorrow. By daybreak the fighting will be over – in fact it may be over already – and then we'll know whether the raiders or the people of Kilfenora have won.'

'I think Kilfenora will win,' said Rory placidly, chewing the last piece of meat from the hind leg of the hare.

'Me, too,' agreed Malachy. 'But if we're both wrong, what do we do then?'

'Easy,' said Rory. 'We bring Mary back to our parents' house, and we go off towards Galway and find the monks at Kilmacdugh. You can join the monks there just as easily, and they're bound to be able to use me for some stone-cutting or repairing.'

Malachy said nothing. There was nothing that he could say. He could not admit that he did not want to leave Mary – but what was there for him to do? He did not know how to farm, he would be useless to Mary's father, and in any case Rory had lots of brothers.

Still, thought Malachy, there's no point in worrying. Rory was right; it had looked as if Kilfenora was getting the best of the battle. Rolling himself in his cloak and holding Xanadu snugly to his chest, he put his head down and fell asleep.

When he woke he could see that it was already daytime. A shaft of sunlight came from the entrance passage, and he could hear the rusty cawing of the grey crows.

Mary and Rory were still asleep, and Malachy decided not to disturb them. There was no point in getting up particularly early, he thought; if the fighting was over then there was no hurry, and if it wasn't, they would be safer in the underground chamber than anywhere else.

Malachy began to think about Colm. Was he really responsible for the raid, he wondered? And if so, was it because of this book? Was the book itself so valuable – or was it perhaps connected with rumours of buried treasure at Kilfenora?

He took the book from the pocket inside his cloak and began turning over its fine calfskin leaves. It truly must be one of the most wonderful books in the world, he decided, not for the first time. As he turned over the leaves he became so immersed in its beauty that he forgot that he was looking for some map or plan of a hiding place for treasure, and he had to start at the beginning and go through it again.

While he was doing this, Mary woke up. In a low voice Malachy told her what he was doing.

'I don't think it will be as easy as that,' Mary said. 'If it were, the treasure would have been found long ago. It will be a hidden secret, something like a riddle perhaps.'

'I see what you mean,' said Malachy slowly, looking at the pink cheek so near to his own. He had an almost overwhelming desire to kiss her.

And then a sudden idea came to him, an idea so exciting and so wonderful that for almost the first time in his life Malachy stumbled over his words.

'Mary, would you – I mean, if I – Well, I know it sounds mad, but would you –' He stopped, took a great gulp of air, and went on more calmly. 'I know

it's a chance in a million, but if I were to find the treasure of Kilfenora, would you marry me?'

At that moment, the most awkward he could have chosen, Rory woke up, stretched himself noisily and got to his feet.

Malachy, however, was not unduly upset. He could see from Mary's flushed cheeks and smiling lips that if he did manage to find the treasure, she would be very happy to marry him.

Rory was not in a romantic mood. As usual, he was hungry, and unfortunately there was no food left; they had eaten all of the hare last night. And the fire had died down. It was time to investigate the outside world, thought Malachy, and in his usual cool way he took charge.

'Mary, you look after Xanadu. He's feeling happier this morning, but don't let him go out or he might try to make his way back to Kilfenora. Rory, look for some more firewood and keep the fire up, but don't go far away. I'm going to go back to Kilfenora and see what has been happening. Mary, do you think that you could also look after the Psalter of King David?'

'You'd best let me go back to Kilfenora, Malachy,' said Rory gruffly. 'I'd be better able to knock a few heads together.'

'No,' said Malachy decidedly. 'It will be better if I go. I run much faster than you and I can hide better. You stay here and look after Mary and Xanadu, and the book, of course.'

He wrapped his cloak around him, went down the passageway and climbed out of the hole into the bright September morning. The storm had gone and the whole landscape had that newly-washed look which comes when the sun shines after days of rain.

It seemed almost impossible that the events of the night had been real, but as Malachy approached Kilfenora, he could see the smoke of several fires rising towards the sky in the windless air.

His heart felt sore and swollen. Had the raiders fired the village? Would he come into a street full of wrecked houses and dead or dying people? At least they haven't fired the abbey, he thought. The spire of the church stood out against the blue sky, and he could see the great bell which he had tolled the night before.

As he drew nearer, he began to feel better. The fires were not as numerous or as great as he had feared; the clear air had made the smoke seem worse than it actually was. He was coming quite near to Kilfenora, and he moved cautiously, keeping in the shadow of stone walls or behind boulders.

He could hear the sound of voices, and then the bell began to toll. One, two, three, he counted; twenty, thirty, forty, fifty; and still the great bell tolled, until it reached seventy-six. Then, in a flash, Malachy understood: they were tolling Brother Mark's death-knell. Seventy-six – that was right; he had been seventy-four when he came to Kilfenora, Malachy remembered.

With no more thought for his own safety, Malachy began to run. Around by the back lanes he went, past his and Rory's house, until he reached the open door of the abbey. As he ran, he could hear the solemn, sweet sound of the monks chanting. '*De Profundis* ...' they sang, and Malachy cared nothing for his own half-broken voice as he joined in with them.

'It was you who saved the abbey, my son,' said the Abbot some time later. 'We would all have been burnt in our beds if you had not tolled the bell. Our good friends and tenants from all around came quickly to our aid, and the only damage has been to a few old houses where the thatch needed renewing anyway. But tell me, did you manage to save the Psalter of King David?'

'Yes, Father,' said Malachy happily. 'It's quite safe, and Rory is looking after it in a secret place.'

'Praised be the Lord,' said the Abbot joyfully. 'And now, my son,' he added seriously, 'you must carry on this great work in memory of Brother Mark. Leave your present work and start today on the Psalter of King David.'

'Father,' said Malachy nervously, 'I have something I must tell you. I think Colm was the one who brought the raiders here. I think they wanted to steal the Psalter of King David.'

The Abbot's face was totally disbelieving. 'Now, my son,' he said soothingly, 'I know that you and Colm have had your differences, but I cannot believe that he would do the abbey any harm. After all, he has been brought up here since he was a baby.'

Malachy said no more, but he made up his mind that he would keep a close eye on Colm.

'I had better go and fetch Mary and Rory, Father,' he said aloud. 'They are still in the secret hiding place.'

'Do, my son,' said the old Abbot gently, 'and then start your work on the Psalter of King David. Work helps sorrow.'

So that afternoon Malachy began the great work of continuing where Brother Mark had left off. He worked with care and with concentration, and from time to time the other monks came in to look at what he was doing. Brother Declan, who was working at a nearby table, took a special interest. When the two were cleaning their brushes at the end of the day, he said, 'You know, Malachy, this must be the most beautiful copying that has ever been done by someone of your age. Even Brother Mark himself, the Lord have mercy on his soul, could not have produced a page as perfect as this one.'

Malachy glowed with pleasure. In the days that followed, he hardly lifted his head from his work, and gradually the memory of the raid, Colm's treachery and the threat to the precious book all slipped to the back of his mind. As he worked, Xanadu lay cosily on his lap; and although Malachy was supposed to make a straightforward copy of the Psalter of King David, from time to time he could not resist painting a triangular face, with slanted eyes of the most vivid blue, peeping from between the upright bars of a capital M.

CHAPTER EIGHT

It was not until a day early in March that Malachy began to discover the answer to the puzzle of the Psalter. It was a very cold day, and the snow fell softly in slanting drifts. The rushes in the fields were still standing up in brownish-green spikes, but the ground below was covered with a dense soft blanket of snow. The cows were bellowing for hay, and even the farmyard ducks were standing around with their eyes shut and their shoulders hunched in misery.

Malachy, Xanadu in his arms as usual, stood with Rory at the door of their house. Rory was his usual cheerful self, delighted with the progress which he was making on the High Cross, but Malachy felt vaguely discontented. Although everyone praised the work which he was doing on the Psalter of King David, he was beginning to feel that he would prefer to create his own thing of beauty rather than copy someone else's masterpiece. For once he felt disinclined to start work.

'I'll come with you, Rory,' he said. 'I'd like to have a look at the cross. I haven't seen it for a long time.'

The two boys pulled the hoods of their cloaks over their heads and walked over to the field. The cross lay on the ground, propped up against a massive stone. Over it, Rory had builT a temporary roof, roughly thatched with bundles of rushes, so that he was sheltered from the worst of the weather; but the snow had blown under this, and the patterns on the cross were outlined in a delicate tracery of white, making them stand out sharply.

'I've finished the side facing the east,' said Rory. 'I've decided to leave the bottom of it without any ornamentation. Soon I'll have finished the west side as well. I've only got the circular design in the centre to do.'

Malachy stood admiring the west-facing side. He could remember the books from which he had copied the patterns: this block from the Gospel of St John, this from the monks' prayer-book, that one from the Gospel of St Mark. At the bottom of the cross there was an empty space, as on the east side; and then, set all by itself inside a triangle, was a strange interlacing pattern.

'Where did I get this pattern from, Rory?' he asked, puzzled. 'It's on the page of the Psalter that I'm copying now, but I never noticed it before yesterday. It's not like the usual patterns in the books in the monks' library.'

Rory stared and then shrugged his shoulders. 'I don't know,' he said. 'You and Mary set out the patterns for me. I just copied them.'

'Yes, I know,' said Malachy slowly. At the back of his mind was the feeling that this matching of patterns was very important, but his mind refused to make the connection for him. Without another word to Rory, he turned and went back towards the Scriptorium, his dark cloak speckled with the flakes of snow, the solid body of the little cat feeling like a hot flask against his chest.

Outside the Scriptorium Mary stood waiting. 'I've brought over some fresh bread for you and Rory,' she said. 'Shall I put it in the house?'

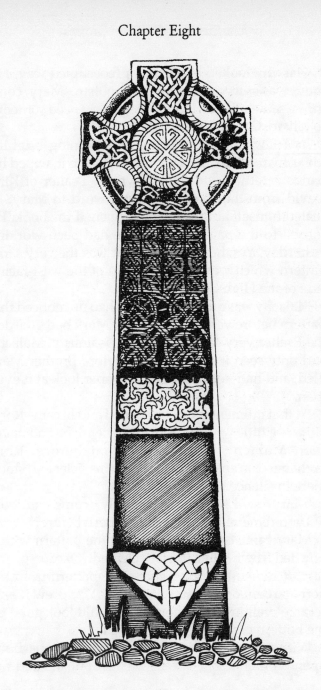

Malachy looked at her in a preoccupied way. His mind was still working on the problem. 'Mary, come in,' he said. 'I'll soon have a fire going. I need someone to talk to. Can you wait for a while?'

In a few minutes the fire was burning brightly. Malachy put Xanadu on the floor next to it, wiped his hands carefully and took down the Psalter of King David from the shelf. Without a word to Mary, he seated himself at the table and opened the book. He turned to the page on which he had been working yesterday. Yes, he was right: that was the very same pattern which was on the bottom of the west-facing side of the High Cross.

Malachy was quite sure that he had not noticed that pattern before yesterday. Brother Mark had guarded the Psalter very carefully, almost jealously. Malachy had only seen it once or twice before Brother Mark died, and had not really had a proper look at it even then.

At that moment the door opened and in came Rory. He was a little worried about his friend; he had never seen Malachy looking like that before. Rory exchanged an anxious glance with his sister and stood there in silence.

'Mary,' said Malachy eventually, 'come and look. Do you remember seeing that pattern before?'

Mary came over and looked at the pattern with a puzzled frown. Then her face cleared. 'Of course,' she said. 'I remember now. That's the pattern from the herb garden, don't you remember? You drew it on a scrap of vellum and I thought it would look good on the bottom of the cross, all by itself.'

Without answering, leaving the precious book open on the table, Malachy dashed outside and ran across the village street. Ignoring the snow, which was falling heavily, he entered the herb garden. Nothing was left of its summer luxuriance, just a few brown stalks sticking up through the snow; but the hedges of box were as thick as ever, and their patterns, with the white icing of snow on top of the leaves, showed up clearly.

Malachy walked to the corner. Yes – how could he have forgotten? There was the same pattern he had found in the Psalter of King David!

When he opened the door of the Scriptorium he was blazing with excitement. He still did not really understand what the connection meant, but he knew that it must mean something. He hung up his wet cloak and then turned again to the Psalter of King David. Carefully he went through the book, finding the strange pattern again and again.

'There's something very peculiar in this,' he said eventually. 'The pattern doesn't fill a whole page, or even half a page. It just seems to be under some words or at the side of some lines.'

Rory and Mary drew nearer and looked at the pages he was indicating.

'It *is* strange,' said Mary. 'It almost looks as if the pattern is there not for a decoration, but to show that a particular word or sentence is important.'

'I'm so stupid,' said Malachy slowly.

'And to think of all those years when you were trying to make me believe that you were clever,' mocked Rory, glad to see his friend look more like himself again.

'Don't you see,' said Malachy, hardly able to speak with excitement, 'the pattern in the nineteenth psalm and the pattern in the twenty-first psalm are both under the same word: *aurum.'*

'And what does *aurum* mean?' asked Rory, catching some of his excitement.

'It means gold,' said Malachy, trying to keep calm.

Mary was busy turning over the pages. 'Oh, but look,' she said with disappointment. 'It's under a different word here in the fifteenth psalm. What does this word mean, Malachy?'

'Don't worry, that word is *pecunia* and it means money. Look at psalm twelve: *argentum.* That means silver, so we're still on the right track. Where did I see that pattern again? Ah, here we are – psalm seventeen. *Abundantia* – that means wealth; and look here, *aurum* again. We have found the secret of the treasure of Kilfenora!'

Trembling with excitement, Malachy flung his arms around Mary and, lifting her up, did a little dance in the middle of the room.

'That's all very well,' said Rory, not showing much surprise at seeing his sister in the arms of someone who until a few months ago had been determined to become a monk. 'That's all very well, but where's the treasure? It's not in a book.'

'But don't you understand?' said Malachy, releasing Mary, a bright flush staining his usually pale cheeks. 'There's only one other place where that pattern occurs. The treasure must be in the herb garden, in the part where the box hedges make the strange pattern.'

The three friends stood in the middle of the room, staring at each other. It hardly seemed possible that they had discovered the secret. They felt almost afraid to go further in case they were bitterly disappointed by finding nothing.

Malachy broke the silence.

'We must go very, very carefully now,' he said. 'We know that Colm is already suspicious. He seems to have picked up the rumour that this book contains the key to the treasure of Kilfenora. His attempt at getting the book stolen came to nothing, and he can't read, so his only chance is to watch us like a hawk. If we make a move he'll be right behind us. If I go anywhere outside the village, these days, he always seems to be following me. In fact, he might be outside the door now.'

Rory moved as quietly as he could to the door, and Mary picked up Xanadu and cuddled him protectively. Rory flung open the top half of the door and glared out, but there was nobody there.

'A bit cold for our friend, today,' he said, closing the door. 'The blacksmith's forge has its door closed. Still, we must be careful. If we ever discuss plans, we must check that no one is listening.'

'Well, I've been talking to Xanadu,' said Mary solemnly, 'and he thinks that Colm will find it most interesting if he sees Malachy – who, as everybody knows, hates gardening – suddenly starting to dig the herb garden in the snow.'

Malachy grinned. Excitement was shooting through his veins; he felt as if something was bubbling inside of him.

'There's only one way to do it,' he said. 'Rory and I must come out in the middle of the night and dig up that section of the herb garden.'

'Oh, that's not fair,' protested Mary. 'I want to be there too.'

'Well, you can't come out here in the middle of the night by yourself,' said Rory with brotherly impatience.

'Xanadu would like me to be here,' persisted Mary. 'Malachy and you will be busy, and you know how terrified he gets if he's left alone. I could hold him for you. I know what we could do. Rory could come home for the night – you know he does sometimes – and then we could come over together just after midnight. I'll be back home again before anyone is up in the morning.'

Malachy's eyes shone with pleasure, and Xanadu reached up with his paw and patted Mary's cheek, as if to say that he approved. Rory had to give in, although he grumbled a little at having to walk over the Burren twice in one night. Malachy, however, was delighted. He had not liked the idea of leaving Mary out of the excitement and the adventure.

'I think we had all better get on with our work, now,' said Rory. 'We don't want Colm to notice anything different about us. Mary, you get back home and tell Mother that I'll be spending the night in the house. You get on with your copying, Malachy, and I'll go back to the West Field.'

At that moment the door opened and in came Brother Declan. He stared inquisitively at the three flushed and excited faces and held the door pointedly open until Mary, with a quick bob in his direction, passed through. Brother Declan, despite all his kindness, was beginning to think that pretty sister of Rory's spent far too much time hanging around the Scriptorium. He hoped that Malachy was not being diverted from his vocation by her. The boy had been looking rather quiet and unhappy recently, and did not seem to take the same pleasure in his work as he once had. However, he did look much better today. There was a glow in his eyes and a flush on his cheeks. Brother Declan gave a satisfied nod to himself and, fetching his work materials and the Gospel which he was copying, settled down at the table.

Malachy got his own brushes and inks from the shelf and set them down with his usual precise movements. He sat on his stool, patting his lap to invite Xanadu onto his usual cosy perch. Dipping his brush into the little pot of gold paint, he slowly and carefully outlined the capital A of *Aurum*. Gold, he thought. Will we really find gold tonight?

CHAPTER NINE

Malachy found it very difficult to go to sleep that night, and when he did eventually drop into an uneasy doze he had strange and terrifying nightmares. He dreamt of a great heap of gold, lying, oddly enough, just inside the door of the bell-tower; when he tried to touch the gold, it turned into a heap of jumbled skulls, and as he drew back in horror, worms began to ooze out of the skulls.

Malachy forced himself to wake up. He sat up in bed, his hair sticking to his forehead and his armpits drenched with sweat. He was afraid that he might have overslept; quickly pulling on his hose and tunic, and leaving Xanadu still curled up in the warm hollow in his bed, he went to the door and opened the top half as quietly as he could.

There was a full moon outside, and Malachy knew from its position that it was about midnight. There was no one around, but Malachy stayed at the door for a few minutes, admiring the way the soft white snow sparkled in the moonlight. It was a frosty night and the dark blue sky was studded with stars. They would hardly need a lantern, thought Malachy; the night was almost as bright as day.

Rory had promised to bring a couple of spades from his father's farm, so there was nothing for Malachy to do but wait. He passed the time by making a hot drink of camomile for the three of them.

Whatever about Rory, Mary would be cold and tired after her walk.

The kettle had barely boiled when there was a gentle tap on the door, and there were Rory and Mary, their faces red from the cold but their eyes glowing with excitement. When they had had their drink, all three went quietly out into the cold night air. Malachy carried the lantern concealed under his coat. They stole along the village street where the moon illuminated the small stone houses.

'I wish it were a bit darker,' whispered Malachy. 'It would be very easy to see us in this bright light.'

'Shh,' said Mary warningly, putting her finger to her lips.

No one said anything else until they were safely inside the gate of the herb garden. This was well away from the houses, so they relaxed a little. Malachy set the lantern on the ground next to the bed containing the skullcap herb. Taking a spade from Rory, he carefully dug up the herb and put it to one side.

'There,' he said, 'that won't come to any harm. This is the dormant season for plants. It doesn't matter about digging them up at this time of year. We can plant it back when we finish.'

'We may not want to bother, once we find the treasure,' said Rory wickedly.

As he said the word 'treasure' there was a sharp intake of breath.

'What did you say?' said Malachy, turning to Mary.

'I didn't make a sound,' said Mary.

'Well, I heard something just as Rory was speaking,' said Malachy, puzzled.

'Oh, let's cut out the talking and start digging,' said Rory impatiently.

'Xanadu is growling,' said Mary suddenly. 'Perhaps that's what you heard.'

Indeed, there were low rumbling noises coming from the little cat, and his tail was swishing from side to side. Malachy stared at him uneasily. 'No, I don't think it was that,' he said. 'It was more like a gasp or something, not like Xanadu's noises.'

'Dig,' said Rory, picking up Malachy's spade and handing it to him.

They dug in silence for ten minutes. The earth was not difficult to dig. For hundreds of years it had been a herb garden, and the soil had been worked all of that time. Between the work of the monks and the work of the earthworms, the earth was deep and soft.

By the end of the ten minutes Rory had dug a huge pile of earth and Malachy a slightly smaller one. Mary looked at the heaps on the path with some apprehension.

'I hope we'll be able to put all this back tidily,' she said in a low voice.

The two boys only grunted. Malachy was beginning to feel rather exhausted, and he was beginning to lose hope. They had dug at least two feet of earth from the whole of the skullcap bed, and still there was no sign of anything. Rory was also beginning to lose hope. He had more experience of digging than Malachy had, and he knew how thin the soil around the Burren is. We must soon come to rock, he thought – and then cheered up when he thought of the hundreds of loads of farmyard manure which must have been placed on top of this bed over the centuries.

Xanadu continued to growl softly, under his breath, and Mary felt quite apprehensive. He had never behaved like this before. It felt as if he was trying to warn them about something. She opened her mouth to say this – when suddenly there was a soft thud and Rory said, in a voice that was almost more frightened than excited, 'I think I've found it.'

The other two crowded forward, and Malachy held the lantern high while Rory continued to dig carefully around a small square object. After a few minutes' work, he leaned down and picked up a small solid box.

'I think it must be made from lead,' he said. 'It would never have lasted in the ground for so long if it had been made from wood; and it feels very heavy.' He held it out to Malachy. 'Go on,' he said, 'you open it.'

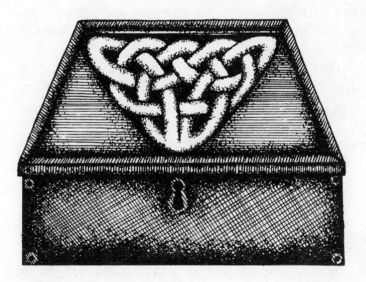

For a few minutes Malachy struggled to lift the lid of the little box, but the latch and the hinges were made of iron, and they had rusted. He could not open it. Rory tried, but he also failed.

'Wait here,' he said. 'I'll go back to my workshop and get a chisel and a crowbar. I won't be long.'

Left to themselves, Mary and Malachy examined the box. It was beautifully ornamented, with intricate designs moulded into it, and with a thrill of excitement Malachy recognised the pattern from the Psalter of King David.

'I didn't expect it to be so small,' whispered Mary.

'Well, it doesn't matter, if it truly is gold,' whispered back Malachy. 'Gold is so valuable that you only need a small quantity of it. We'll give half to Rory and we'll still have enough to get married on. Let's not have a farm. I shall make beautiful books and sell them if our money runs out, and you will sew or spin or pick flowers or do whatever you want to do.'

They sat there hand in hand, dreaming happy dreams, until the noise of panting told them that Rory was back.

'I had a lucky escape,' whispered Rory. 'The blacksmith had his half-door open and he was looking out down the street. I just managed to duck behind the house and come around by the lane. That's why I was so long.'

Malachy wondered briefly what the blacksmith was doing looking out of his door in the middle of the night, but he soon forgot about it. He and Mary watched, almost bubbling over with excitement, as Rory carefully prised up the lid of the little lead box.

They had no need of the lantern. The full moon shone almost as brightly as the sun and its light was magnified by the whiteness of the snow, but even still, again and again, Malachy flashed the lantern's light into every corner of the box, vainly trying to see whether anything had been overlooked. It was empty.

At least, it was empty except for a key.

'A key,' gasped Mary.

'A key,' echoed Rory.

Malachy said nothing. His throat was swollen with disappointment and misery. He had been so sure .... He stood and stared at the box, turning it over and over in his hands.

From behind him came a sharp sound. Malachy wheeled around and in the moonlight saw clearly why Xanadu had growled.

There stood Colm, just behind them, staring into the box. He did not attempt to hide; he just flung his head back and began to laugh out loud.

'Ha, ha!' he laughed, his broad teeth very white in his sooty black face. 'And you thought you would find treasure and get married! Well, the sight of your faces was worth getting up in the middle of the night for, I suppose, but the next time you go hunting for treasure try to find something a bit more exciting, won't you?'

His laugh did not last long, however. Rory, glad of an opportunity to relieve his feelings, flung himself on Colm and started to punch and pummel him.

Mary stood there feeling rather sick. She hated fights. That was one of the reasons she liked Malachy so much. He was always so gentle. She was sick with disappointment, too. All their dreams ending in a key .... Even if it had once opened something, it was probably over two hundred years old and the door it unlocked would be long gone.

'So you just clear off and don't let me see your ugly face anywhere near me again,' Rory was saying to the sobbing Colm. 'Oh, and by the way, your father is looking for you. With a bit of luck he'll give you another hiding.'

Smearing the blood from his nose, Colm limped off towards the street. Rory turned to Malachy. 'I think you should come back with me and Mary,' he said seriously. 'That Colm will be in a nasty mood, and he might pay you a little visit later on. Let's just put the earth back, and then we'll be on our way.'

CHAPTER TEN

The next day the snow melted and the endless rain began again. Malachy worked grimly on at his copy of the Psalter, and Rory began cutting the patterns in the circle on the top of the west-facing side of the High Cross. Rory was not as upset as the other two. He was one of those lucky people who enjoy life and enjoy their work. He would have liked gold, but it did not matter to him in the same way that it mattered to Malachy and to Mary.

Mary was completely miserable. Her jobs, milking cows and collecting eggs, did not occupy her mind, so she brooded continually about that moment when the beautifully-engraved lead box had been opened and there had been nothing in it but a huge iron key. Who would hide a key so carefully? she thought. There must be some reason.

'You see, Malachy,' she said a couple of weeks later, when they were walking together around the little farm of Drumshee, looking for early marsh orchids, 'you see, it doesn't make sense. There *must* be some connection between the key and the treasure of Kilfenora. Perhaps we shouldn't give up so easily. Perhaps we should try the key in some of the doors at the abbey.'

Malachy looked at her with a glimmer of hope in his eyes. 'Mary,' he said, 'the night we went into the herb garden, I had a strange dream. I dreamt that I went into the bell-tower and there was some gold there, but then it turned into a heap of skulls, and worms came out of the eyes and ears.

Mary shuddered but said in her usual practical way, 'Well, I don't really believe in dreams, but we have to start somewhere. Why not the bell-tower? Let's not bother about the marsh orchids any more. I think it's too early anyway.'

The village street was deserted when they got back. The morning services were over in the abbey, and there would be no more until Compline. The monks were all having a rest after their best meal of the week, and Rory was showing one of his brothers his work on the crosses. The blacksmith's fire was out, as always on this sacred day of rest. Nevertheless, Malachy was uneasy.

'I think you should stay on guard outside the abbey, in case Colm is spying on us,' he told Mary. 'If he appears, start singing at the top of your voice and I'll come out straight away. Let's just collect the key from the box. Rory and I hid it in the thatch. We were afraid Colm might decide it was interesting, after all.'

A few minutes later Malachy disappeared inside the bell-tower and Mary was left outside, scanning the street for any sign of Colm's ugly face. Will Malachy find anything? she wondered. She could hardly bear to think about it; she was too afraid of being bitterly disappointed again. He won't find anything, she repeated to herself again and again; but it was no use. When Malachy reappeared and she saw the disappointment on his face, her own spirits plunged as deeply as if she had been sure he would find the treasure.

'Well, the key doesn't fit the door there,' he said in a casual voice which she knew was disguising his disappointment. 'I went up the steps and all around. There are no doors, other than the main one, and the key is the wrong shape for that. It would have to be something completely hidden, anyway. Remember, the treasure has probably been hidden for two hundred years. It would have been discovered by now if it were anywhere obvious.'

At that moment Colm came out of the blacksmith's house and looked at them suspiciously. 'Thinking of ringing the bell again, Malachy?' he taunted. 'After all, the monks rely on you to keep saving them.'

'And on you to keep betraying them,' snapped Malachy, who was very much out of temper with this second dashing of his hopes.

Colm doubled up his fists, but in the distance came the sound of Rory's booming laugh, echoed by the even louder laughter of his three elder brothers, so Colm decided not to answer. He was pleased to see Malachy looking so depressed. Colm was beginning to lose hope of finding the treasure of Kilfenora; and yet that man from the Tipperary clan seemed to be quite sure that the old book held the secret, and he was paying Colm good money to keep watching Malachy.

'We'd better have a look around the church,' said Malachy to Mary in a low voice. 'We don't want him poking around the bell-tower yet, in case I missed something. We can come back later, when he's gone.'

'Very well,' said Mary in a low voice – and then, aloud, 'Let's go and pray for Colm at the tomb of St Fachtnan.'

Colm's eyes darkened with anger and his cheeks flushed, but he turned away without a word. The two friends laughed and went over towards the church.

Inside, the church was cool and dim. They wandered about and came to a stop by the tomb of St Fachtnan, in the chancel at the top of the church.

'I wonder who carved this?' said Mary idly, kneeling down to look closely at the tomb. 'I don't think he was as good as Rory, do you? Look at the book he's holding. It hardly looks like a book, does it?'

'Well, Brother Declan thinks it might be a chalice,' said Malachy, 'but Brother Mark was sure that it was the Psalter of King David.'

'His neck is too long, also,' went on Mary critically, 'but the face is quite good and I like his little hat.'

'That's a skullcap,' said Malachy absentmindedly, his attention fixed on the book.

As soon as he said the word 'skullcap' Mary rose to her feet, her blue eyes wide and startled. At the same moment the same thought came to Malachy. He stood staring at her, his breath coming in quick short pants.

'Shh!' said Mary, her finger to her lips. Her quick ears had caught a sound, and Malachy heard it also. It was a creak – just the slightest one, but they knew they had been followed. At that moment a shaft of sunshine came through the west window and lit up the burly figure of Colm.

'Why, Colm,' said Malachy, 'we just don't seem to be able to get rid of you today. Is there anywhere we can go where you won't come following us?'

'Let's go,' said Mary. 'We'll find Rory and the others. We'd better start walking back to the farm.'

Colm turned and without a word went out of the church, slamming the door loudly behind him.

'Here's our opportunity,' said Malachy quickly. 'He won't dare to come back for a while, and in any case he knows that we can hear the door if he does. Let's think. This must mean something. Let's get all the facts clear.' He thought for a moment, his brain rapidly sorting through the facts, and then held up his left hand and started to count on his fingers:

'One: The key was buried within a pattern identical to the one in the Psalter of King David.

'Two: The pattern in the Psalter of King David clearly shows up words like "gold" and "silver".

'Three: This carving of St Fachtnan is supposed to have the Psalter of King David in his hands.

'Four: St Fachtnan is wearing a skullcap.

'Five: The herb in that section of the herb garden is called skullcap.'

Mary smiled admiringly. She had thought of all this herself in one flash of understanding, but only Malachy would be able to set all her confused thoughts out so clearly.

'There must be a connection,' she said firmly.

'The trouble is that I can't see any sign of a door near the tomb, can you?'

'Perhaps it's not a door, perhaps it's a chest,' suggested Mary.

'Wait a minute,' said Malachy suddenly. 'I have an idea.'

He knelt down on the floor and touched the strange little skullcap with his sensitive fingers, tracing the carved lines on it and then feeling carefully all around the rim. Suddenly he gasped.

'What is it?' whispered Mary.

'I thought something moved there for a second. Let me try again.'

Once again he moved his fingers around the
rounded edge of the skullcap, digging into the dirt of
centuries with his fingernails. This time he was sure.
The skullcap had moved.

He tried again, but he could not get it to move more than a fraction of an inch.

'It definitely is moving,' he said to Mary in a low voice, 'but my fingers aren't strong enough. Do you think it's possible for you to send Rory to me and keep the rest of your brothers talking? Slip out by the north door and go down Well Lane. Colm won't see you then – and anyway, it's me that he keeps an eye on.'

Without a word Mary went out the north door, shutting it carefully and quietly behind her. Two minutes later Rory came through the same door. In a whisper, Malachy told him what he and Mary suspected.

Rory took his chisel from its pouch on his belt. He carefully scraped away the dirt and slid the chisel under the edge of the carving. For a moment nothing happened. Rory exerted more pressure, straining, the veins on his forehead standing out like whipcord – and then it happened. With a suddenness which almost threw Rory off balance, the skullcap came off and revealed a large keyhole.

Malachy took the old iron key from his pocket and, with trembling hands, tried it in the lock. It fitted perfectly.

'Quick,' he said, his mind working rapidly and clearly, 'quick, put it back. We can't do anything now. We must plan carefully. Let's go and find Mary. And don't show any excitement. Colm is probably skulking about somewhere. Above all, he must not find out about this.'

It was hard for Rory not to show excitement. He put the skullcap back carefully, so that there was no sign of the disturbance, but he wanted to shout or turn somersaults or dance a jig in the middle of the church.

Malachy, however, felt a deadly calm come over him. He felt certain that they were very near to finding the treasure of Kilfenora, and he did not want anything to come between him and that treasure.

Walking back across the Burren, Malachy discussed the matter with Mary in low tones. Ahead of them Rory was working off his high spirits by wrestling with one of his brothers, and their shouts and yells made a perfect cover for the planning.

'We must choose a night with no moon,' said Malachy, 'and we must be very careful that we're not followed this time. I'll get the key of the church from Brother Declan. I'll make up some excuse. Then we'll be certain that no one can spy on us.'

Before they parted they decided that they would try a week later, when the moon was new, and that, if possible, they would choose a cloudy night. Malachy would go home with Mary and Rory. This would not be a problem, as Rory's mother was very fond of Malachy and was always inviting him to stay. If they were together they could creep into the village from the north side, well away from the blacksmith's shop, and get into the abbey without any risk of being seen.

It was only when he was going home, later on that night, that Malachy thought of his dream and remembered the skulls. He wondered what they would find beneath the saint's skullcap, but he pushed his anxieties away from him and set his shoulders resolutely. This time, he thought, we must not fail.

CHAPTER ELEVEN

It was almost a fortnight later when the three friends set out on their night of adventure. During those two weeks the nights had been clear and frosty, and although the moon had been only a crescent for the week before, the stars had been so bright and the heavy frost had reflected their light so much that Malachy had decided it would be unwise to try. Both Rory and Mary were worried that someone else might get there before them if they delayed too long, but Malachy was grimly determined that this time there would be no mistakes.

'After all,' he said, 'it has stayed there for about two hundred years. It can wait another week.'

It was more than ten days before the rain returned. At last it came, sweeping in from the ocean in torrential downpours.

'This will last a week,' said Brother Declan, eyeing the sky in the late afternoon. 'When you get rain with a southwesterly wind at this time of year, it always takes a while to go away again. I think I will finish now, my son. This weather makes my old bones ache. I shall go and see Brother David. He has promised me some oil of rosemary to rub on my legs. What about you, Malachy? Will you stop now? You have just got to the end of that psalm and it would be a good place to finish.'

'Yes, I might,' said Malachy, trying to keep his voice calm and indifferent. 'If you give me the key to the church, I'll lock it after Compline for you and open it for Matins.'

Brother Declan's face lit up with gratitude. 'That is kind of you, Malachy,' he said. 'I feel old and weary tonight. I think I will ask Brother David if he can spare me a bed in the infirmary. Quite a few of the other monks are there already with this fever. There won't be many at Compline this evening.'

Malachy looked at him sharply. Brother Declan did indeed look very tired. 'Are you well, Brother?' he asked with concern.

'Oh, yes.' Brother Declan forced a smile. 'I'm just worried about the abbey. So many abbeys and monasteries around the West have been raided. Ever since that night when you saved us, I keep thinking that they will come back in much greater numbers. I dread the thought. I am too old for battles.'

He shook his head sadly, handed Malachy the massive keys to the church and walked slowly and painfully away. Malachy tucked the Psalter into his pouch, picked up Xanadu and locked the door of the Scriptorium.

Rory was coming down the street; and lounging against the door of the forge was Colm.

'Is tonight the night that your mother asked me to come and stay with you, Rory?' he asked.

Rory picked up the cue as fast as lightning and replied without hesitation.

'Of course it is, you fool. Don't let Mary know that you almost forgot. She'll have been baking for the last few days to get ready for you.'

'Well, we'll have to wait until after Compline,' said Malachy in the same light tone. 'I promised Brother Declan to lock the church for him.'

Chapter Eleven

Rory gave him a delighted wink. Everything seemed to be working out.

It was a splendid night for the attempt. The moon was completely hidden, and although it was not raining the sky was full of clouds. The three friends made their way cautiously into the village by the north street. Rory held a crowbar in one hand, in case they needed it either for levering up the slab or for protection. In his other hand he held the covered lantern just inside his cloak, ready to give a gleam of light whenever it was needed. Mary had some spare candles and a tinder box and flint. Malachy, as usual, had Xanadu inside his cloak. He felt quite weighed down: in his pouch were the Psalter of King David, the key to the church and the enormous iron key they had dug out of the herb garden.

The village street was completely dark. Not a light gleamed under any doorway, not a single fire flickered. In dead silence they made their way to the church. The darkness was so complete that they could not see the door, and Malachy ran his hands along the wall, as a blind man would do, until he felt the rough, nail-studded wood of the door.

Shifting Xanadu to his left arm, he pulled the key to the church out of his pouch and turned it in the lock as silently as he could. The heavy lock made a grating sound as he turned it – a sound which he had never noticed before, but which sounded horrifyingly loud in the silence of the night. They all stayed still, afraid to move, but not a sound came from the village street; no voice was raised, no door was opened.

Malachy began to breathe again. He slipped into the church; beside him he could hear Mary's soft breathing and Rory's heavy footsteps. He pushed the heavy door closed and turned the key in the lock once more.

Only then did Rory dare to show a gleam of light. He held the lantern under his cloak and half-opened the shutter, so that a faint beam fell on the floor and they could see their way to the tomb of St Fachtnan.

'Now,' said Malachy in a whisper, 'Colm can't disturb us this time.'

Rory placed the lantern on the ground next to the tomb, and they all knelt down. In tense silence, Rory took his chisel from his belt and levered the little skullcap off of the carved stone figure. Mary gave a gasp of excitement when she saw the keyhole, but the other two were still full of tension. What would happen if the lock had rusted and would not turn?

Rory dropped a little grease carefully into the hole and then took the key from Malachy. Exerting all his strength, he twisted the massive iron key.

The lock creaked and groaned, but it turned. Little by little, it moved. Rory was afraid to exert too much pressure in case the lock broke, so he did not rush it. The other two could not see much movement, but Rory could feel that it was turning.

At last there was a final clank and Rory stood up.

'I think it's open,' he said. 'The next question is: what does open?'

Malachy had an inspiration. 'Perhaps the entire slab is like the lid of a chest,' he said. 'Maybe it's hinged and it can be raised.'

'Let's try it,' said Rory. He took the crowbar and scraped away the dirt from all around the slab, and tried to lever it up on the north side. Nothing happened.

'Try the other side, the south side,' said Malachy, in a low voice which trembled very slightly. Rory moved around to the south side and tried again. Nothing happened.

'It's unlikely to open on one of the short sides,' he said, staring at the slab in a puzzled way.

Malachy could have cried with frustration. Were they always to be disappointed at the last moment? He looked at Mary with despair in his eyes.

'Let's not give up,' she said quickly. 'We lose nothing by trying the other two sides.'

Rory shrugged his shoulders. 'Well, what's your choice? West or east?'

'East, of course,' said Malachy, forgetting to whisper in his excitement. 'After all, the keyhole is at the east. And people are always buried with their heads pointing towards the east, because that's where the sun rises, as a sign that they'll rise again from the dead.'

Rory picked up the crowbar again and scraped the dirt away from the eastern side. For the third time he inserted the crowbar. Malachy held Xanadu close and buried his face in the cat's soft warm fur. He could not bear to look.

But he did not need to look. With a loud creaking and grating, the massive slab rose from the ground.

CHAPTER TWELVE

alachy had thought that they might see a tomb filled with bones, or perhaps a massive stone chest, but they found neither of those things. They saw a flight of stone steps, leading down into what looked like a passageway.

'Let's go down,' said Mary eagerly.

'Wait a moment,' said Rory cautiously. 'I'm going to close it again and see if Malachy can open it. If he can, I'm going to go down and check if it can be opened from the inside.'

They tried it out, and Malachy glowed with pleasure when he found that he was strong enough to lever up the slab. Rory left him the crowbar and climbed into the hole, pulling the slab shut behind him.

Malachy and Mary held hands, feeling suddenly quite frightened without Rory's solid presence. They need not have worried, however: two minutes later the slab opened again and there was Rory.

'That's it, then,' he said. 'No problem. We'll take the key with us, and if by any chance someone gets into the church before we're back, no one will know we're down here and no one can lock us in.'

He handed Malachy the key to put back in his pouch, and carefully replaced the little skullcap over the keyhole.

Mary went first, Malachy next. Rory manoeuvred the slab until it was almost in position, and then he too slid in carefully. The slab clanged shut above them.

The three looked at each other. In the light of the lantern their faces were pale. Without saying a word, they went one by one down the stone steps.

Quite soon they reached the end of the steps, but there was still nothing to be found. There was no room, no treasure, just a long passage paved with stone and roofed with stone slabs.

'Which direction do you think we're going in, Malachy?' asked Rory in a low voice.

'West, I should imagine,' returned Malachy.

'That's what I would have guessed too,' said Rory. 'In fact, I should think we're about under my western stone cross at the moment.'

'Where can it be leading to?' asked Mary, her heart beginning to sink.

Malachy looked at her and nodded his head. 'I'm beginning to wonder,' he said gravely. 'Maybe there's no treasure here; maybe we've discovered a way out of the abbey which the monks used to take in times of danger. I have a feeling it may come out at that old ruined fort a hundred yards to the west of the stone cross.'

'I can't believe it,' said Rory robustly. 'Too many things have pointed us to this place. We must find something.'

The other two said nothing. In a way, because the treasure mattered more to them than it did to Rory, they found it almost unbearable to keep hoping and talking about it.

It would have been better if we'd never heard the word 'treasure', thought Malachy savagely. I can't bear any more disappointments.

Chapter Twelve

Silently, one behind the other, they went down the passage. It was intensely dark, and Rory kept the light of the lantern directed on the moss-covered flagstones. We must have walked about a quarter of a mile by now, he was thinking – when suddenly he stumbled and almost sent the lantern flying.

'What is it?' cried Malachy, who was just behind him.

'Don't know,' grunted Rory. Then, flashing his light on the ground, he gave a quick whistle. 'It's a step up,' he said; 'and look,' he added, raising the lantern and sweeping its light around the walls.

Mary and Malachy followed the direction of the light, and both drew in a breath of excitement. They had reached the end of the passageway and were in a small square chamber, obviously built under the ruined fort west of Kilfenora.

'It's a souterrain,' said Malachy, the fresh hope which was rising within him reducing his voice to a hoarse whisper. Without another word he took the lantern from Rory and held it high, sweeping its light over every inch of the floor, then over the rough walls, and finally, in desperation, over the smooth slabs of stone which formed its ceiling.

There was nothing there. No chests, no casks, not a single place where treasure could be hidden.

Malachy sat down on the wet ground and leaned his head against the wall. The other two watched him in silence. Malachy was always the leader, but now in the dim light of the lantern they could see that the confidence had gone from his face and his cheeks were wet.

Rory hardly liked to look at him. Picking up the lantern, he walked around the floor, admiring the professional way in which the stone flags had been cut into perfect rectangles and laid with perfect joints. Did they use some sort of mortar in those days? he wondered, bending down and running his broad forefinger along the edge of a slab.

It was as he was doing this that the other fingers of his hand felt something rough. To anyone other than Rory this roughness would merely have felt like cracks, but Rory knew instantly that these were no random marks; these were the deliberate work of a chisel.

He lifted the lantern and examined the corner of the slab carefully. There definitely did seem to be something there. Taking his own chisel from his belt, he scraped the dirt away. By now Mary was kneeling beside him.

'What is it?' she said in a whisper.

'It looks like a drawing of the sun,' said Rory. 'I wonder why it was put there.'

Malachy took a deep breath and, with difficulty, got himself back under control. He got up and came across to the other two. 'I think it might be the tomb of St Fachtnan. I've been wondering where he was buried, since he wasn't under the slab in the chancel.'

'Well, let's have a look,' said Rory cheerfully. 'Hold the lantern for me, Mary, will you? Malachy, can you help me scrape away the dirt around the edge? These stones fit very tightly together.'

They worked in silence for about ten minutes. Then Rory took the crowbar, levered the slab up and, taking it in his two hands, turned it over to rest on the ground beside them. Mary lit the lantern and shone it into the hole.

Malachy had been right. The bones of a man lay there, one arm by his side, the other raised to point above his head. Below his feet was a stone slab, and on the slab were engraved some words. Malachy bent over, tracing the grime-filled letters with his finger.

'Funny,' he murmured, 'I would have expected his name or else some long inscription. This seems to be just four words. Lend me your chisel again, Rory.'

Malachy carefully worked the dirt out of the engraved letters, and Mary knelt beside him, holding the lantern so that its light fell on the words. When they were finally clear, Malachy read the message twice over to himself before his voice was steady enough to read it to his companions.

'It's written in Latin,' he said. 'It says: *Si aurum requiris, superspice.* That means: If you want the gold, look above.'

Mary said nothing, but directed the light of the lantern to the stone ceiling above them.

'No,' said Rory quickly. 'Look at the way the hand is pointing. It must mean the slab above the head of St Fachtnan.'

Without bothering to clear the dirt away from the side of the slab, he seized the crowbar and levered up the massive piece of stone.

And this time they were not disappointed. There, under the slab at the head of St Fachtnan's bones, was a hollow stone-lined enclosure; and within it were six large jars of the type that was used for holding wine or oil. Each jar was filled to the brim with gold coins. Next to the jars stood four beautiful chalices, made from gold and studded with jewels. The treasure of Kilfenora had been found.

CHAPTER THIRTEEN

The three friends stood gazing into the stone-lined space beneath the slab. Nobody said a word. Mary thought that she must scream or laugh or cry or do *something* to break the terrible tension; but Xanadu was the one who did that. Attracted by the flash of lantern-light on the gold coins, he leapt from Malachy's arms and landed neatly on the rim of one of the large jars. With a deft paw he fished inside it and neatly flipped out one of the gold pieces. Malachy picked it up. It had the head of a man on it, a man with a clean-shaven face and very short hair. Beneath the face was an inscription in Latin. He turned it over, looking at it with wonder, until Xanadu gave an indignant miaow and tapped his paw on Malachy's hand.

'He wants his share,' cried Mary, exploding into hysterical laughter.

'Probably thinks they're some tasty kind of fish,' said Rory, his deep chuckle ringing through the stone chamber.

Mary picked up Xanadu and held him to her cheek, her lips touching the warm silkiness of his fur. 'We'll buy you a fine leather collar studded with jewels,' she promised, 'and you'll have a silk cushion to lie on. After all, you must have your share, too.'

Malachy turned and looked at her. 'Talking about shares,' he said, 'who exactly does this treasure belong to?'

'To us, of course.' Rory, at least, had no doubt about it.

Mary said nothing, but looked enquiringly at Malachy. He had the look of someone who is wrestling with his conscience.

'You see,' he said, 'in a way, this treasure may have an owner and the owner may be the monks of Kilfenora.'

'I don't see how,' said Rory simply. 'After all, even if monks originally buried it, that must have been hundreds of years ago. It was lost and forgotten and we discovered it. I think it belongs to us.'

'I'll tell you what we should do,' said Mary, eager to prevent a quarrel. 'We should tell the Abbot the truth and give him the four chalices – after all, they're worth more to him than to us. And then we should offer him a fair share of the gold coins. I don't know much about coins, but there certainly must be enough there for everybody.'

Malachy breathed a sigh of relief. Trust Mary to come up with a good solution, he thought. Rory was nodding in agreement. 'These gold coins might be enough to make the whole of Kilfenora rich,' he said. 'What on earth are we going to do with them all?'

'Well,' said Malachy, 'that's another good reason to tell the Abbot the truth. We may need to get them changed into smaller coins, and we'll certainly need to keep them safe. We can hide them in the underground room at Drumshee and just take them out when we need them.'

'But what will we use them for?' persisted Rory.

Malachy paused. All his secret dreams were about to come true, and he was shy about revealing them.

He took a deep breath. When the words did come, they came out in a rush.

'I was thinking that you could engage a team of masons and workmen and build us a castle. Brother Mark was telling me about castles that he saw out in the east – like big towers, he said, with rooms one on top of the other and a great winding staircase joining them.' He stopped and smiled to himself as he remembered all the wonderful visions that Brother Mark had described: the walls hung with silken cloths and woven pictures and painted leather hangings, and the rooms full of precious books with calfskin bindings.

'We could build it in the *cathair* at Drumshee,' he continued, 'on top of the underground room. Mary and I and you and Xanadu could all live there, and we could store our gold in the underground room.'

'I'll build a castle for you and Mary, certainly,' said Rory with a grin, 'but I can't say that I fancy living with you two lovebirds. I'll build myself another castle down the hill from you, just where the River Fergus curves around that rocky little hill, and I'll spend all my days fishing. I'll buy myself a couple of giant wolfhounds, and they can guard my share of the treasure.'

They all stood there for a few minutes, dreaming happy dreams. Then, with a sigh, Malachy shook himself slightly.

'Well, in the meantime,' he said, 'we'd better be getting back. We must be sure to replace everything exactly as it was, and not to come here again until I've had a chance to talk to the Abbot. We must remember that the danger from Colm and his friends is a very real one. We could still lose all of this.'

The others nodded in agreement. Soon the two slabs were back in place, and, picking up the lantern, Malachy led the way back down the passageway. Mary followed with Xanadu in her arms, and Rory came last.

They had almost come to the bottom of the steps when Mary spoke in a low voice. 'Malachy,' she said, 'stop for a minute. I don't know what's the matter with Xanadu. He keeps struggling to get out of my arms, and he's trembling.'

Malachy stopped and shone the lantern on Xanadu. The little cat was indeed trembling. He was trying to escape from Mary's arms – not as if he wanted to be carried by Malachy, but as if he was trying to escape back down the passageway again.

'He's twitching his nose as if he can smell something,' said Rory, puzzled. He hesitated and then added, 'I think I can smell something, too.'

They all stood still, breathing deeply through their noses. Malachy's eyes met Mary's and he nodded. 'It's definitely a smell of burning. You two stay here. Don't let Xanadu go, Mary. I'll just creep up the steps and put my ear to St Fachtnan's slab and see whether I can hear anything.'

Mary and Rory stood quite still until Malachy rejoined them. His face was pale in the light of their lantern. 'Something terrible is happening,' he said in an almost soundless whisper. 'I heard screams and yells, and the church is definitely on fire. I could hear the roaring of the flames, and the slab was warm. Let's get back to the underground room as quickly as possible.'

They turned and fled down the passageway, but they had only gone about a hundred yards when a dreadful exploding noise, like thunder, came from behind them. When they looked back, they saw that a giant boulder had slid down and was completely blocking their path.

'That probably makes it safer for us,' said Rory, once the noise had subsided a little. 'No one will ever be able to come down that passageway again, and there's bound to be a way out at the other end.'

Malachy nodded, and at a slightly slower pace they made their way back to the underground room. Rory was right. By some tumbled stones, overgrown with ivy, there were the remains of a broken stone staircase.

'Give me Xanadu, Mary,' said Malachy in a low voice. 'Hold on to my cloak and be careful not to slip.'

Rory went first, breaking off branches of the goat-willow bushes which choked the steps and pushing aside the long stems of bramble which were as thick as a man's arm. Malachy followed, doing his best to shield Mary from the worst of the thorny growth. Xanadu, luckily, was now relaxed and calm. Even though the smell of burning was overwhelming, he seemed to sense that they were no longer going in the direction of the fire, and he stayed quite calm even when they reached the open air.

Scrambling out of the hole, they turned to face the east and saw that the whole sky was lit up – not with the light of the morning sun, but with the fierce glare of a hundred fires. It was not just the abbey which was burning; the whole village of Kilfenora was on fire. Thatched roofs burned like tinder, limestone walls exploded, and the air was full of the raiders' cries of triumph and the wails and moans of the defeated.

Malachy's face was white with shock. He no longer felt any joy or triumph at the thought of the treasure. His one concern was for the lives of the gentle monks who had taken him in as a homeless orphan, fed him, clothed him and taught him everything that he knew.

'I must go back,' he said hoarsely. 'I must try to do something.'

'Have some sense!' said Rory. 'What on earth can you do? And what can I do, for that matter? If we go running down the street of Kilfenora we'll just get ourselves killed, as well.'

Malachy did not answer. He was thinking hard. Almost absent-mindedly, he handed Xanadu over to Mary and clambered back down to the underground room. Rory pulled a few of the goat-willow branches over the hole again, in case anyone was passing, and then he and Mary followed.

Malachy had left the room by the time they arrived; he was out in the passageway, holding up the lantern.

'Oh, good,' he said, as they arrived. 'I thought I might find this and I was right. Look down there.'

'It's another passageway,' said Mary.

'But it's not going back to the church,' said Rory. 'This one must be going south or south-west.'

'Yes, of course,' said Malachy confidently. 'That's what I expected. You see, we were right: this passage was an escape-way, probably long forgotten, for the monks to get safely out of the church. And if they had one from the church, the chances are that there was also one leading from the guest house and the hospital. I'm sure that's where this is going.'

'You may well be right,' said Rory doubtfully. 'That doesn't alter the fact that you are leaving this nice safe place and going back to the fighting.'

'I must,' said Malachy stubbornly. 'If there's any hope of rescuing Brother Declan and any of the other monks, then I have to try.'

'Well, if you must, you must,' said Rory resignedly. 'I'd better come with you to stop you getting into too much trouble.'

'No,' said Malachy firmly. 'You stay here. This is my idea and my responsibility. I won't take any unnecessary risks.'

'We'll come with you,' said Mary, just as firmly. 'It's no good us standing around here in the cold twiddling our thumbs. You may be wrong; there may not be a way out to the guest house and the hospital. Then we can just come back here and keep ourselves safe until all the fighting is over.'

Malachy hesitated and then nodded. Carefully they made their way down the southwestern passage. It ran along in a straight line for a few hundred yards, and then started to climb steeply uphill. Malachy nodded to himself with satisfaction. This was what he had expected. The guest house and the hospital were on slightly higher ground than the abbey. It looked as if his idea might be correct after all.

'It feels quite cool and fresh in here,' whispered Rory. 'Do you think we might be coming to the way out?'

'I wouldn't have thought we were as near as that,' whispered back Malachy, 'but there might be some sort of air-hole in the roof. There must be some way for air to get in, or it would be dangerous.'

As fast as he dared, he went down the uneven stone passage, with Rory and Mary close behind him. Rory was carrying the lantern. He held it as high as he could, in order to give Malachy light, but Malachy was too impatient and too worried about Brother Declan to go carefully; he hurried beyond the circle of light from the lantern, confident of his footing. That confidence was misplaced: the next moment he fell heavily over some stones scattered on the ground, and his outstretched hands met what seemed to be a solid wall of stone and earth and tangled ferns.

'Oh, Malachy, have you hurt yourself?' whispered Mary.

Malachy got to his feet with an effort and flexed his leg. For a moment he was afraid that he had broken it, but it seemed that it was only badly bruised. He took a deep breath.

'I'm all right,' he said, shortly. He knew that he had been stupid. He should have let Rory lead the way with the lantern.

'Well, we seem to have found where the air is getting in,' said Rory, lifting the lantern and flashing its light around.

They stopped and stared upwards, their eyes straining through the gloom. For a moment they could see nothing, but then a gust of wind must have blown the clouds away from the moon. Suddenly they could see it – a pale half-circle of light above them, seen through a tangle of twisted thorn-bushes.

'I can see what's happened,' said Rory. 'There must have been a time when the monks had two ways of escape down to that underground room. But over the years the knowledge of the way down through St Fachtnan's tomb was lost, and this way was blocked by the roof breaking and the stone falling. Probably everyone has forgotten that the passageway used to lead somewhere.'

'It might have happened in an attack a few hundred years ago,' said Mary. 'Maybe all the monks were killed, so there was no one left who knew where the treasure was hidden and that this escape-way existed.'

'I know what probably happened,' said Malachy, forgetting all his bruises in the excitement. 'Probably one monk escaped and wrote down the secret of the treasure in the Psalter of King David, so that the knowledge wouldn't be lost.'

Rory wasn't listening. He had carefully placed the lantern on the floor behind him, and, with muscles well trained by years of working with stone, he was moving the huge boulders to one side.

'Good job they're limestone,' he grunted. 'If they were bluestone or greenstone, like at Drumshee, they'd weigh twice as much.'

Malachy thought about offering to help, but decided that he would be of more use if he held the lantern up so that Rory could see what he was doing. He was dying of impatience, because now he was quite sure that this passage must lead to either the hospital or the guest house, but he knew that Rory was working as hard as he could.

One by one the huge boulders were moved, and the earth was thrown aside, until at last Rory gave a grunt of satisfaction.

'That's it,' he said. 'We're through.'

Malachy held up the lantern and moved forward eagerly. Then he gave a cry of surprise. They were not in a continuation of the passageway, as he had expected, but in another underground storeroom – and this one was not empty. It was full of people, all looking at them with frightened faces; people dressed in long robes, with cowls over their heads. All the monks of Kilfenora were hiding in this underground place. The Abbot was there, and so were Brother Declan and Brother David and all the others, packed together as tightly as cattle in a cart, their faces pale with terror.

'Thank God,' whispered Brother Declan. 'I thought it sounded like you, my son. How did you get here?'

CHAPTER FOURTEEN

And so the story of Malachy and Rory and Mary and the monks of Kilfenora ended happily.

The monks found refuge in the monastery of Kilmacdugh until the raiders had finally disappeared. Malachy went to live with Rory's family, and when he was sixteen, he and Mary were married.

Malachy used some of his gold to buy four thousand acres of land around Drumshee, and Rory kept his word and built a magnificent castle for Mary and Malachy in the fort on top of the hill. There was a huge kitchen with a fireplace big enough for ten fires, a vast dining hall, a solar or sitting room for Mary, and many luxurious sleeping chambers; and right at the top of the tower, well away from any danger of thieves or fire, there was a library for Malachy's books. Outside the castle, but within the defensive outer wall, Rory built a row of stables, and next to them were two large gateposts from which hung a pair of massive iron gates. A long avenue lined with young oak trees swept up the hill to these stately gates.

In a cosy corner of Mary's sitting room was a basket lined with a silken cushion, and on wet or windy days Xanadu, the royal cat of Siam, lay there with the firelight winking on his jewelled collar. On fine days, however, he hunted joyously around the nearby farmyards; and in the years to come, many of the kittens lurking around the cottages near Drumshee had bright blue eyes, tall pointed ears and strangely kinked tails.

One of the first things Malachy did after the treasure of Kilfenora had been shared out was to find out what had happened to his two brothers. They were alive; the cattle raiders had sold them into slavery, but Malachy had more than enough gold to buy their freedom. They came back to Drumshee and managed his land for him; Malachy kept his promise never to become a farmer. He and Mary travelled overseas and brought home beautiful books for Malachy's library, and all their children grew up able to read and write.

Rory did build a castle on the banks of the River Fergus. He called it Inchovea, and he did indeed have a happy time there with his wolfhounds and his fishing. He did not live there alone, however: shortly after the castle was built he married Bridget, one of Malachy's cousins.

Although they all lived in great luxury, the treasure of Kilfenora seemed endless. Malachy buried a purse of gold; and Rory carved the secret of the hiding place into the east side of the great stone cross which still stands outside the cathedral of Kilfenora.

There is only one more thing to tell in the story of Malachy, Mary and Rory. When Rory was building Mary and Malachy their wonderful castle, he turned the old underground room into the castle cellar. To make the mortar that held the stones together, he and his men used mud from the old well. One day Mary and Malachy were standing at the edge of the new cellar, watching the work; suddenly, as a bucket of mud was flung down into the cellar, Mary cried out in amazement.

'What is it?' asked Malachy.

'I thought I saw a gold chain – a necklace, I think!' said Mary. 'There, in the mud!'

Both Malachy and Rory laughed.

'She can think of nothing but gold these days,' said Rory, with a wink at Malachy.

Mary said no more. She thought she had made a mistake.

If she had insisted, she might have discovered the gold necklace which had lain for centuries deep in the mud; but she did not. It was another three hundred years before it was found.

NUALA & HER SECRET WOLF

The Drumshee Timeline Series: Book 1

Cora Harrison

Fergus, an orphaned wolf cub, is Nuala's secret – and
her dearest friend.

Everyone in her Iron Age world hates and fears wolves,
and she knows that if her father finds Fergus, he will kill
him.
So she feeds him, plays with him and trains him to track
and herd – in secret.

But there is danger, and not only for Fergus.
Cattle-raiders are watching the fort – and their leader
wants Nuala for his bride.

Can Fergus save Nuala and her family?

Warm, fast-paced, rich in historical detail,
Nuala & her Secret Wolf is a story to enchant animal
lovers everywhere.

ISBN 0-86327-585-0

**Watch for the next book in the
Drumshee Timeline Series!**

WOLFHOUND PRESS
68 Mountjoy Square
Dublin 1
Tel: (+353 1 8740354) Fax: (+353 1 8720207)